THE FORSAKEN LACEMAKER OF HAMPSTEAD

RACHEL DOWNING

CORNERSTONETALES.COM

FAMILY BREAKFAST

$\mathcal{S}$unlight crept through the lace curtains, casting intricate shadows across Mabel's face. She blinked away sleep, watching the delicate patterns dance on the wooden floor of their cottage bedroom. The familiar shapes reminded her of the stories her mother wove into each design—flowers for hope, circles for eternity, leaves for growth.

The floorboards creaked beneath her feet as she slipped from beneath the warm quilts. Through the doorway, dried flowers hung in neat bundles from the kitchen rafters—purple lavender, white daisies, and golden yarrow. Their faded perfume mingled with the morning air. Mother's latest lace designs adorned the walls, each piece telling its own tale. A collar with intertwined roses spoke of summer gardens, while a shawl's pattern echoed the flight of swallows.

"Time to rise, sleepyhead," Mary called from the kitchen. The gentle clatter of dishes accompanied her voice.

Mabel selected a simple cotton dress from the chest, its fabric soft from many washings. She pulled it over her head, smoothing the wrinkles with practiced care. Though she was only nine, her fingers worked swiftly, separating her chestnut hair into three sections.

Mabel padded across the worn floorboards toward the kitchen, where her mother bent over her work table. Threads and bobbins scattered across its surface caught the morning light. The smell of fresh bread embraced her, mingling with the earthy scent of dried flowers and starched lace.

Her sister, Emma, sat at the corner of the table, her small tongue poking out in concentration as she traced flowers across the pages of her sketchbook. Her chubby five-year-old hands were surprisingly dexterous. Her bright blue eyes darted between the dried blooms hanging above and her emerging artwork. Her other sibling, Henry, squirmed in his chair beside her, more interested in creating towers from his wooden bowls than eating his breakfast.

Two-year-old Henry smacked two wooden bowels together in delight. Emma's musical giggle filled the air.

Mabel reached for the family's prized tablecloth, her fingers tracing the delicate pattern Mary had created for her wedding day. Each stitch told a story—lilies for love, roses for beauty, ivy for faithfulness. She spread it carefully across the table, smoothing away invisible wrinkles.

Thomas' heavy footsteps announced his arrival. He filled the doorway with his presence, already dressed for teaching in his well-worn but carefully pressed coat.

Thomas settled into his chair, his eyes twinkling as he cut into his bread. "You wouldn't believe what young Timothy did yesterday." He leaned forward, drawing the children closer with his conspiratorial tone. "He brought a frog to class, hidden in his slate."

Emma's eyes widened. "What happened next, Papa?"

"Well, this frog had quite different ideas about arithmetic. It hopped straight onto Miss Martha's copy book!"

Henry clapped his hands, spilling crumbs across the precious tablecloth. Mary reached over to brush them away, her fingers lingering on Thomas' sleeve. Their shared glance spoke volumes —years of love and understanding passing between them in a single moment.

After the plates were cleared, Mabel watched her father arrange his books on the kitchen table. His fingers traced the spines with reverence—Shakespeare, Milton, even a battered copy of Robinson Crusoe that had seen better days.

"The older students are ready for poetry," he mused, showing Mary a page marked with neat annotations. She nodded, suggesting passages that might capture young minds.

"What's this word mean?" Emma appeared at Thomas' elbow, pointing to a page in her own book. "'Mag-nif-i-cent'?"

"Ah!" Thomas' face lit up. "It means something grand and beautiful—like your mother's lace, or the sunset over Hampstead Heath."

Emma tried the word herself, stumbling over the syllables. Henry, watching from his perch on Mary's lap, waved his arms in imitation of her careful gestures, sending both siblings into fits of giggles.

Mabel's heart swelled as she watched her father guide Emma through the pronunciation. His patience never wavered, his joy in teaching as evident here at their kitchen table as it was in his classroom. In their modest cottage, filled with books and lace and love, she understood how knowledge could transform the simplest moments into something precious.

A FINE DAY'S WORK

*T*hrough the window, Mabel watched her father's figure grow smaller as he strode down the path toward the village school. His leather satchel swung at his side, packed with the morning's chosen books. With it being Saturday, he didn't need to head into work, but he ran extra sessions for students who were struggling. The school couldn't afford to pay him for it, but he did it simply out of the generousity of his heart. He truly cared about all of his students.

Mary settled at her work table, pulling a delicate piece of lace toward her. Her fingers danced across the fabric like water over stones, each movement precise and purposeful. The morning light caught the silver threads woven through the pattern, making them shimmer like dewdrops on a spider's web.

"The countess requested peonies," Mary murmured, more to herself than anyone else. Her needle flashed as she added subtle details to the blooming flowers taking shape beneath her hands.

Emma crept closer, her eyes wide with wonder. "Can I help, Mama?" She reached out to touch the lace, then pulled back, remembering her mother's rules about clean hands.

"Come here, darling." Mary patted the chair beside her.

"First, we must check the threads for tangles. See how they catch the light? That tells us they're properly aligned."

Emma's small fingers copied her mother's movements, carefully separating the fine strands. Her face scrunched in concentration as she worked.

Henry bounced on his toes nearby, snatching up bits of loose lace that had fallen to the floor. "Me help too!" He clutched his treasures to his chest, sending a cascade of white scraps floating through the air like snow.

"Careful with those, my little magpie." Mary's laugh filled the cottage. She reached out to ruffle his hair as he scampered past, still gathering his collection of fallen pieces.

"Look! I found! Look!" He held up a length of ribbon, tangled hopelessly with three bobbins and what appeared to be yesterday's bread crust.

Emma giggled, covering her mouth with her hands. "Henry, that's not lace!"

"Lace! Lace! Lacey lace!" He waved his prize in the air, sending the bobbins spinning.

Mabel wiped her hands on her apron, the morning's dishes finally cleared and dried. The familiar scent of lavender soap lingered on her skin as she joined her family at the work table. Mary had cleared a space in the center, where an ornate wooden box lay open, its velvet lining deep as midnight.

"The countess will want this displayed at her spring garden party." Mary lifted the lace with reverent hands. Light danced across the intricate pattern – peonies unfurling their petals amid delicate leaves and stems. "Each flower tells a story."

Emma pressed close to the table's edge, her eyes following Mary's fingers as they traced the design. "Like the stories in Papa's books?"

"Just so." Mary smiled. "See how these petals overlap? That shows life flowing from one season to the next, like the tales we pass down."

Henry bounced on his toes, pointing to a particularly complex section. "I winded for that!"

"You did indeed." Mary's eyes crinkled with pride. "And Emma chose which flowers to include in the border."

Mabel carefully lifted the tissue paper, letting it float down to cushion the box's bottom. The paper whispered against the velvet, a sound as soft as secrets shared between sisters. She held her breath as Mama lowered the lace into place, each fold precise and deliberate.

"Your grandmother taught me these patterns," Mary said, smoothing the corners. "She learned them from her mother, who brought them from France." Her hands stilled for a moment. "Now I teach them to both of you."

Mabel tucked the final layer of tissue over the lace, securing their family's artistry in its bed of paper and velvet. The box's lid closed with a gentle click, like the period at the end of a cherished story.

"There," Mary breathed. "Perfect as a prayer."

THE EVENING SHADOWS stretched across the cottage walls as Mabel settled onto the worn rug near the hearth. Emma tucked herself against her side, while Henry sprawled on his stomach, a stubby pencil moving across the pages of his treasured notebook.

Thomas pulled his favourite leather-bound volume from the shelf, its spine cracked and softened from years of loving use. The book fell open naturally to well-visited pages of Wordsworth. Mary's hands stilled over her lace as she listened, needles gleaming in the firelight.

"'I wandered lonely as a cloud,'" Thomas began, his voice rich and measured. The familiar words filled their small home like music. Emma pressed closer to Mabel, her eyes wide with wonder at the dancing daffodils painted by their father's voice.

Henry's pencil paused mid-stroke. He glanced up at Thomas, then back to his paper where stick figures cavorted across the page. Mabel noticed how he tried to match their movements to the rhythm of the poetry.

Thomas' voice faltered slightly as he turned the page. "There's been talk at the school," he said, marking his place with a finger. "The new leadership has... different ideas about how things should be run."

Mabel caught the quick exchange between her parents — her mother's fingers tightening around her lace bobbins, her father's shoulders tensing beneath his worn jacket. Unspoken words hung in the air like dust motes in the firelight.

Emma shifted against Mabel's side, sensing but not understanding the sudden heaviness in the room. Henry's pencil scratched more slowly across his paper, his usual energy dampened by the change in atmosphere.

"From what I've heard, a real change won't come for years, my love. Perhaps we should return to the poetry," Mary suggested softly, her hands resuming their dance with the lace. But Mabel saw how her mother's typically steady fingers trembled slightly as they worked the delicate patterns.

Thomas cleared his throat and found his place again in the book. As he resumed reading, Mabel noticed how his knuckles whitened against the leather binding, though his voice remained steady and warm.

THE ARRIVAL OF MR ARDON

*M*orning dew still clung to the grass as Mabel and Emma walked beside their father toward the village school. Now fifteen, Mabel was coming close to the end of her time at this school, but she adored it. Emma had started when she turned six, and little Henry was just about to start, next week!

The familiar path wound past gardens bursting with late summer blooms, their sweet scent mingling with the crisp air. But today, something felt different. The usual chatter of children and parents fell silent as a tall figure appeared at the school gates.

Mr Ardon's shadow stretched across the cobblestones like an ink stain. His face pinched into sharp angles, as if carved from cold marble. He stood motionless, watching the arriving families with steel-grey eyes that seemed to catalog every detail, every flaw.

Mabel's father squared his shoulders and nodded a greeting. "Welcome to Hampstead, Mr Ardon."

Mr Ardon's gaze swept past Thomas without acknowledgment, his lip curling slightly as he surveyed the modest schoolyard. Parents drew their children closer, whispering behind raised hands. Mrs Cooper, who'd always praised Thomas' teaching of her three boys, dropped her eyes to the ground when Mr Ardon's attention turned her way.

Inside the assembly hall, wooden benches creaked under rows of fidgeting students. Mabel sat with her class, her back straight despite the knot forming in her stomach. The morning sun filtered through high windows, catching dust motes that danced around Mr Ardon's severe silhouette.

"Father looks so small up there," Mabel thought, watching him stand to one side of the platform. His familiar kind face, which had guided countless children through their letters and sums, seemed to fade beneath Mr. Ardon's looming presence.

A wave of whispers rippled through the room as Mr. Ardon stepped forward. "Quiet," he snapped, though no one had spoken above a murmur. His voice cut through the air like winter frost.

Mabel's hands clenched in her lap as Mr Ardon's gaze swept over her father with naked disdain. She recognised that look – the same one worn by fine ladies who sometimes passed her mother in the street, noses lifted high as if detecting something unpleasant.

MR ARDON'S boots clicked against the floorboards as he paced the classroom. Mabel's chest tightened as he paused behind her father, who was explaining the properties of triangles to the younger students.

"Perhaps, Mr Fairchild, if you spent less time with flowery analogies and more time drilling proper mathematics, these children might actually learn something of value." Mr Ardon's words sliced through her father's lesson.

Thomas' chalk hesitated mid-stroke. "The children respond well to—"

"They respond well to discipline and structure." Mr Ardon snatched the chalk from Thomas' hand. "Not fairy stories about shapes dancing in gardens."

A few students giggled nervously. Mabel had to hold in the tears she could feel welling at the corners of her eyes.

"Now then." Mr Ardon erased her father's careful drawings with sharp, angry strokes. "Who can recite their multiplication tables? Quickly now."

Thomas stepped back, his shoulders slumping as Mr Ardon took command of the classroom. The children's voices shook as they rattled off numbers, flinching each time Mr Ardon's chalk cracked against the board.

"Pathetic," Mr Ardon spat. "Mr Fairchild, your students lack even basic mathematical comprehension. I expected better from someone who claims such extensive teaching experience."

Mabel's fingers dug into her palms as she watched her father absorb the insult, his face flushing red while Mr Ardon continued his tirade. The morning sun that usually warmed their classroom now felt harsh and exposing, highlighting every crack in the floorboards, every frayed thread in her father's coat.

DAY'S END

*M*abel watched her father push the potatoes around his plate, his fork scraping against the ceramic in a way that made her wince. The usual warmth of their evening meals had vanished, replaced by a heaviness that pressed down on them all.

"Perhaps if you spoke with him directly," Mary's voice carried the softness she used when handling her most delicate lace. "Find common ground in your dedication to the children's education."

Thomas' shoulders slumped. "The man takes pleasure in undermining everything I've built. Today, he questioned my arithmetic methods in front of the entire class."

Emma's spoon clattered against her bowl. Henry reached for it, but his small hands trembled, spilling soup onto the tablecloth.

"Here." Mabel dabbed at the spreading stain with her napkin, grateful for the distraction from her father's defeated expression.

Mary laid her hand over Thomas' clenched fist. "We must

handle this with care, like threading a needle through the finest lace. Too much force, and everything tears."

"What would you have me do?" Thomas' voice cracked. "Stand idle while he destroys years of work?"

Mabel's chest tightened as she watched her mother's fingers intertwine with her father's. The gesture reminded her of the intricate patterns in Mary's lace – delicate yet strong, holding everything together.

Thomas exhaled, his breath heavy enough to flutter the candle flame. The shadows it cast danced across the walls, making the cottage feel smaller than usual. Emma pressed closer to Mabel's side, while Henry stared at his bowl, his soup growing cold.

The silence stretched between them like a thread pulled too taut. Mabel remembered countless evenings filled with poetry and laughter in this very room. Now those memories felt distant, fading like the day's light through their window.

After dinner was complete, Mabel helped clear the dishes, the familiar routine offering comfort against the evening's tension.

Emma tugged at her sleeve. "Will you tell us a story tonight?"

"Your father will pray for you, my loves," Mary gathered Henry into her arms. "But I think it will be straight to sleep tonight. He's had a very long day."

They climbed the narrow stairs to their shared bedroom, the wooden steps creaking beneath their feet. Thomas knelt beside their beds, his voice steady despite the strain Mabel noticed around his eyes.

"Dear Lord, watch over our family as we sleep. Guide us through troubled times with wisdom and grace." His hand found Mary's.

"Sweet dreams, my darlings." Mary kissed each child's forehead, lingering a moment longer over Henry's tousled hair.

Mabel lay still in her bed, listening to Emma's breathing

slow beside her. The floorboards outside their door groaned as her parents descended to the kitchen. Their voices drifted up, muffled but clear enough for her to catch fragments.

"...the school funds..."

"...cannot prove anything..."

"...his accusations..."

Mary's voice trembled. "If they investigate—"

"Hush, love. We must trust in—"

Their words faded as they moved deeper into the house. Mabel pulled her blanket tighter, the wool scratching against her chin as she stared into the darkness. The familiar shadows of her bedroom now seemed to hold secrets she'd rather not know.

WHISPERS

*M*abel's heart pounded as she hurried Emma and Henry home from school, the whispers of other children burning in her ears. The morning's events replayed in her mind — Mr Ardon's thunderous voice echoing through the assembly hall as he announced the missing repair funds, his cold eyes fixed on their father.

"Thief," someone hissed as they passed the baker's shop. Mrs. Turner, who always saved them day-old bread, pulled her curtains shut.

Emma stumbled on a loose cobblestone. "Why won't anyone look at us?"

Mabel gripped her sister's hand tighter. "Keep walking."

"But Father wouldn't—" Henry's voice quavered. It had been his first day at school.

"Of course he wouldn't!" Mabel spun around, her voice sharp enough to make both siblings flinch. She softened her tone, kneeling before them. "Listen to me. Father taught us that truth matters above all else. Remember how he showed you the difference between right and wrong, Henry? How he helps you sound out difficult words, Emma?"

Their small faces turned up to her, eyes wide with confusion and hurt.

"Mr Ardon is wrong." Mabel's fists clenched at her sides. "Father would never steal — not a single penny. He's spent years making sure every child in that school had books to read, even using his own money sometimes."

"But everyone believes—"

"Everyone is wrong!" The force of Mabel's words scattered a group of sparrows from a nearby fence. She drew her siblings close, feeling their trembling bodies against hers. "Father is the most honest man in Hampstead. Mr Ardon may have fooled the village, but he cannot fool us. We know who our father is."

As the day went on, things got worse. Through the cottage window, Mabel watched Mrs Bennett cross the street to avoid passing their gate. The woman who'd taught her Sunday school for years now clutched her shawl tighter, as if the mere proximity to their home might taint her reputation.

"The Turners sent back Mother's lace." Emma's voice cracked as she held up the carefully wrapped package. "They said they found someone else."

Mabel took the bundle, recognising the intricate flower pattern their mother had labored over for weeks. The same design that had once drawn gasps of admiration at the church fair now returned unwanted, unmarked except for a hastily scrawled note declining the commission.

In the parlour, Mary hunched over her work table, her fingers trembling as they traced familiar patterns. The thread caught and snagged, creating uneven loops where there should have been delicate swirls. She pulled out the mistakes with shaking hands, leaving tiny holes in the fabric.

"Let me help, Mother." Mabel reached for the tangled mess.

"I can manage." Mary's voice wavered. She pressed her palms flat against the table, trying to still their tremors. "The Countess will want her order soon."

"The Countess canceled this morning." Mabel couldn't keep the bitterness from her voice. "Her maid delivered the message."

Mary's shoulders slumped. Outside, voices drifted through the open window — Mrs. Winters and Miss Thompson discussing the school funds in carrying whispers.

"Such a shame about Thomas," Miss Thompson's voice cut sharp as a knife. "Always seemed so respectable."

"The quiet ones are the worst sort," Mrs. Winters replied. "Mr Ardon says the evidence is quite clear."

Mary's hands dropped to her lap, the fine lace thread pooling like tears on the floor. Down the street, the church bells rang, marking the hour their father usually returned from teaching. But Thomas wouldn't be coming home tonight – they'd taken him away that morning, his wrists bound as Mr Ardon watched from the schoolhouse steps.

SENTENCE

*T*he courtroom's wooden benches creaked under the weight of spectators. Mabel sat rigid between Emma and Henry, their small hands clutched in hers as character witness after character witness spoke of their father's integrity.

"Thomas Fairchild taught my son to read when others said the boy was too slow." Mr Cooper, the blacksmith, stood tall despite his soot-stained clothes. "He stayed after hours, never asked for a penny."

Mrs Davis, who sold vegetables in the market, recounted how Thomas had paid for books for children whose families couldn't afford them. Even old Mr Williams testified about Thomas' careful accounting of school funds over the years.

But Mr Ardon's evidence loomed larger than their words. The ledger entries he presented, the missing receipts, the carefully crafted story of deception — all of it wove a net that tightened around Thomas despite his protestations of innocence.

The judge's face remained impassive throughout, his wigged head nodding occasionally as he made notes. When he finally looked up, his eyes swept past Thomas without seeing him.

"The evidence presented leaves little room for doubt." The

judge's voice boomed through the hushed courtroom. "Thomas Fairchild, you have betrayed the trust of this community and the children in your care. I hereby sentence you to fifteen years in Maidstone Prison."

The gavel crashed down.

Maidstone Prison was miles and miles away. There was no chance they would ever be able to visit their father...

Emma's fingers dug into Mabel's arm. Henry buried his face in her side, his small body shaking with silent sobs. Mabel pulled them closer, her own tears falling freely now as she watched two guards approach their father.

Thomas stood straight-backed, dignity intact even as the sentence fell upon him like a physical blow. His eyes found them in the crowd, full of love and sorrow.

Mabel wanted to scream, to rush forward, to make them understand how wrong they were. But she could only hold her siblings tighter as the guards led Thomas away, their father's footsteps echoing against the courtroom's stone floors.

The guards allowed them a few moments in a small room off the main corridor. The space felt too cramped for such an enormous goodbye. Mabel's heart pounded as Thomas gathered them all into his arms, the chains at his wrists clinking against Mary's lace shawl.

"My loves." Thomas' voice cracked. He pressed his lips to Mary's forehead, her face buried in his shoulder. "I will hold you in my heart every moment."

Emma reached up to touch his cheek, her small fingers tracing the lines of worry that had deepened there. Henry clung to his father's leg, refusing to look up, his shoulders shaking.

Mabel watched her mother's hands smooth Thomas' collar, adjusting it one last time as she had done every morning before he left for school. The familiar gesture made Mabel's throat tighten.

"Papa." She stepped forward, fighting to keep her voice steady. "I'll take care of them. I promise."

Thomas cupped her face in his hands, the metal of the chains cold against her skin. "My brave girl. You shouldn't have to—"

"Time's up." The guard's voice cut through their bubble of grief.

Mary's fingers twisted in Thomas' shirt. "Thomas, I—"

He kissed her quickly, desperately, before the guards pulled him back. Emma lunged forward, but Mabel caught her around the waist. Henry's wail echoed off the stone walls as Thomas was led away.

"I love you," Thomas called over his shoulder. "Remember that. Always

remember—"

The heavy door closed behind him, leaving them alone with their tears and the hollow space where he should have been. Mary sank to her knees, gathering Henry and Emma close. Mabel wrapped her arms around all of them, feeling the tremors of their grief shake through her own body.

They stayed like that, huddled together on the cold floor, until another guard came to tell them they had to leave.

VANISHING WORLD

The cottage creaked with emptiness in the days after Papa's sentencing. Mabel watched her mother's hands shake as she unfolded another returned package — this one from Lady Ashley, who had commissioned a christening gown.

"Perhaps there's been a mistake." Mary smoothed the crumpled note that accompanied the return. Her voice caught. "She's ordered from us for years."

But there was no mistake. The package joined a growing pile — each one representing a canceled order, a lost income, another crack in their already fragile world. The Countess' peony lace lay forgotten in its wooden box, the spring garden party long past.

At night, Mabel took her mother's place at the lace table, working by candlelight on the few remaining commissioned pieces. Her fingers moved swiftly through the intricate patterns Mary had taught her, even as her eyes burned with exhaustion. The steady click of bobbins filled the silence where Papa's poetry readings used to be.

Emma and Henry slept nearby on a makeshift pallet —

Mabel had moved them closer to the hearth when they could no longer afford coal for the upstairs rooms. Henry whimpered in his sleep, and she paused her work to smooth his hair, humming softly until he settled.

During the day, she stretched their dwindling supplies, turning yesterday's bread into today's pudding, watering down the soup until it was little more than broth. She darned socks, patched clothes, and tried not to notice how her mother's cough grew worse or how her mother's eyes seemed to look through them rather than at them.

"Just a few more rows," Mabel whispered to herself, returning to the lace. Her mother's words echoed in her mind: "Each pattern tells a story." This one spoke of desperation, of fingers working past pain, of a girl trying to hold her family together one delicate thread at a time.

The candle guttered, casting strange shadows on the wall. Mabel blinked hard and kept working. She couldn't afford to rest – not with the rent due and Emma needing new shoes and Henry's coat too thin for the coming winter. Not with the fear of separation lurking in every empty cupboard, every unpaid bill.

Mabel noticed the cough first — a small, persistent thing that crept into her mother's voice like a thief. Mary tried to hide it behind her hand or muffle it in her shawl, but it grew louder with each passing week. The sound followed her through the cottage, punctuating the silence between words, between breaths.

At the lace table, Mary's fingers trembled more often now. The intricate patterns that once flowed effortlessly from her hands became a struggle. Sometimes she would stop mid-stitch, her chest heaving with effort, and Mabel would quietly take over while her mother rested.

"Look, Mama." Emma padded across the floor, clutching her latest drawing. "I made the garden how it used to be, with all the flowers." She held up the paper, showing bright splashes of colour where peonies and roses once bloomed before they'd sold the seeds for food.

Mary smiled, though the effort seemed to drain her. "Beautiful, darling." Her words dissolved into another coughing fit.

Henry appeared with a cup of water, his young face pinched with worry. "I got it myself," he announced proudly, carefully steadying the cup as Mary took it with shaking hands.

Mabel watched them orbit around their mother like anxious stars, each trying to help in their own way. Emma filled pages with drawings – scenes from happier times, portraits of their family whole and smiling. Henry followed Mabel through her daily tasks, insisting on carrying the lighter baskets of laundry or fetching wood for the stove.

"I can do more," he'd protest when Mabel took the heavier items from him. But she saw how he watched their mother's declining strength with frightened eyes, how he tried to fill spaces too big for his young shoulders.

At night, after Emma and Henry were asleep, Mabel would often find Mary at the window, gazing out at the dark garden. Her mother's frame, once sturdy and capable, had grown as thin as the lace she crafted. The moonlight carved deep shadows beneath her cheekbones, highlighting the pallor of the consumption's steady advance.

Mabel traced her fingers along the delicate edges of her mother's wedding tablecloth, each loop and twist a testament to her mother's mastery. The morning light filtered through the threadbare curtains, casting patterns across the cherished piece from better days — when Papa's voice filled these rooms with poetry and Mama's skilled hands created beauty instead of trembling with fever.

She'd wrapped the tablecloth in oilcloth to protect it from dust and damp, keeping it hidden beneath her thin mattress. Sometimes at night, she would unfold it carefully, letting her fingers follow the intricate patterns until she could almost hear the echo of laughter from their last family dinner before everything changed.

The shame pressed down on her chest like a physical weight. Yesterday, Mrs Cooper had crossed the street to avoid them, pulling her daughter away as if poverty might be catching. The baker's wife had placed their stale bread on the counter's edge, refusing to meet Mabel's eyes or touch her coins directly.

The cottage walls, once warm with family portraits and pressed flowers, now seemed to close in around them. Empty spaces gaped where they'd sold furniture piece by piece. The parlor where Papa had taught them letters stood bare except for Mary's lace table — the last remnant of their former life they refused to part with.

Mabel's fingers found a particular section of the tablecloth where the pattern formed delicate peonies, her mother's signature design. She remembered watching Mother create it, her hands dancing between bobbins as she explained how each flower told its own story. Now those same hands could barely hold a teacup steady.

A tear splashed onto the lace, and Mabel quickly dabbed it away. She couldn't afford such weakness, not when Emma and Henry looked to her with questioning eyes, not when Mama needed her strength. Carefully rewrapping the tablecloth, she tucked it away — a treasure preserved from their vanishing world.

LONDON'S PROMISE

*M*abel's eyes opened before the sun could touch the horizon. The cottage's darkness held only the faint glow of her candle, its flame dancing across the worn floorboards. She pulled herself from the thin mattress, her bones aching from yesterday's work. The wooden box of bobbins clinked softly as she lifted it, settling it on the lace table where her mother had once reigned.

Her fingers, already callused at sixteen, found the familiar rhythm. Thread whispered through her hands as she began the morning's work. The pattern emerged slowly — a delicate edge of roses that some shopkeeper might deign to purchase. No signature peonies today; those belonged to her mother's golden reputation, now tarnished by scandal.

A cough echoed from the back room. Mabel set down her bobbins and padded across the cold floor to her mother's bedside. Mary's face, hollow in the candlelight, turned toward her daughter.

"Let me help you sit up, Mama." Mabel's arms encircled her mother's shoulders, feeling the sharp edges of bones through her nightdress. She adjusted the pillows, poured fresh water, and helped her mother sip slowly.

In the kitchen, Mabel stretched their dwindling supplies. She cut the bread thin, spreading it with the last of the jam to make it more filling for Emma and Henry. Between stirring porridge and stoking the stove's dying embers, her hands returned to the lace. A few moments here, a pattern there — every spare second counted toward their survival.

The bobbins clicked like quiet prayers in the pre-dawn stillness. Mabel's shoulders hunched over her work, mirroring her mother's familiar pose. But where Mary's movements had once flowed like water, Mabel's rushed with necessity. Each twist of thread meant another meal, another day they might keep their home.

Mabel crept back into the bedroom, where Emma and Henry huddled beneath threadbare blankets. Her hand brushed Emma's cheek. "Time to wake, love." Emma's eyes fluttered open, already alert despite the early hour. Henry stirred beside her, curled tight against the morning chill.

"Breakfast is ready." Mabel helped them dress, her fingers working quickly through Emma's tangled hair. The familiar motions echoed that of their mother's gentle touch, now weakened by illness.

In the kitchen, she settled them at the table before returning to Mary's bedside. Her mother's breathing came shallow and quick, each rise of her chest a visible strain. Mabel poured steaming tea into their last uncracked cup, supporting Mary's head as she guided it to her lips.

"Small sips, Mama." The broth followed, though Mary managed only a spoonful before turning away. Mabel tucked the blankets closer around her shoulders, hiding her worry behind a practiced smile.

Back in the kitchen, Emma hunched over a scrap of paper,

her charcoal stick moving in hesitant strokes. Mabel paused behind her chair, studying the emerging pattern.

"Look at these curves here." Mabel traced her finger along a piece of lace draped nearby. "See how they flow like water? Try capturing that movement in your sketch." Emma's face brightened at the guidance, her hand growing more confident.

Henry stood on tiptoe beside them, carefully arranging their remaining dishes. The plates rattled in his grip as he placed them one by one, his lower lip caught between his teeth in concentration. A cup slipped, but Mabel's hand shot out to catch it before it could fall.

"Well done, Henry." She squeezed his shoulder. "You're becoming quite the helper." His chest puffed with pride, though his fingers still shook as he laid out their worn silverware.

Mabel tucked the last crust of bread into Emma's pocket, smoothing her sister's threadbare shawl. "Remember to check on Mama every hour. If her cough worsens--"

"I'll send Henry to fetch the doctor." Emma's chin lifted with determination, though her eyes betrayed a flicker of worry.

"Good girl." Mabel pressed a kiss to her sister's forehead, then bent to ruffle Henry's hair. "And you, keep the fire stoked just as I showed you."

Her worn coat hung by the door, patches carefully sewn over the worst holes. Mabel wound her scarf tight, the wool scratchy against her neck. At the bedroom door, she paused. Her mother's chest rose and fell in shallow breaths, her face pale against the pillow. The morning light cast shadows beneath her sunken cheeks.

The bitter wind hit like a slap as Mabel stepped outside. Her boots, the soles worn paper-thin, offered little protection from the slush-covered ground. Each step brought a fresh surge of icy water through the cracks.

London loomed ahead, a grey smudge against the horizon.

Mabel clutched her precious bundles of lace closer, protected from the wet by layers of oilcloth. Her fingers ached with cold despite her mother's old gloves, the tips poking through frayed openings.

The road stretched endless before her, rutted with cart wheels and horse hooves. Dirty snow piled in drifts along the edges, turning to treacherous slush under her feet. Other travelers passed – merchants with loaded wagons, farmers bringing produce to market – but none offered a ride to a lone girl with worn clothes and determined eyes.

Mabel's jaw set as she pressed forward. Five miles meant nothing if it meant keeping food on their table, medicine in their cupboard. Responsibility settled familiar on her shoulders as she picked her way through the muck, London's promises and perils growing clearer with each step.

LONDON SHOPS

*T*he grimy streets of London pressed in around Mabel as she clutched her bundle of lace closer. Shop windows gleamed with silk dresses and jewelled combs, a stark contrast to her mud-splattered hem. Her reflection ghosted past in the glass — pale face, threadbare coat, eyes too old for her years.

The bell above Madame Beaumont's Millinery tinkled as Mabel pushed open the door. Warmth and the smell of steam-pressed fabric washed over her. Fine hats perched on pedestals like exotic birds, their feathers and ribbons catching the morning light.

"Yes?" A shop girl's voice cracked like a whip. Her gaze swept Mabel from worn boots to windblown hair.

Mabel's fingers trembled as she unwrapped the first piece of lace. The delicate pattern emerged like frost on a window pane – peonies and leaves dancing across cream-coloured thread.

"I've brought some pieces for consideration." Her voice came steady despite her racing heart. "Each one hand-crafted using traditional techniques passed down through generations."

The shop girl's lip curled. "Madame doesn't purchase from street vendors."

"Please." Mabel laid out another piece, this one featuring intertwining vines. "Look at the precision of the stitches, the complexity of the design."

Moving down the street, Mabel entered shop after shop. Some dismissed her outright. Others examined her work with pursed lips before declaring it "unsuitable for our clientele." At Harrison & Sons, the owner squinted at her through his spectacles.

"Beautiful work," he mused, running weathered fingers along the edge of a collar. "But without proper references..."

Mabel's throat tightened. She thought of Emma's hollow cheeks, Henry's too-short sleeves. Squaring her shoulders, she pulled out her finest piece — a handkerchief bordered with tiny roses.

"The technique is Brussels point de gaze," she explained, the familiar terms steadying her voice. "Notice how each petal catches the light differently. The thread count is exceptionally fine, allowing for detailed shading within the design."

The shopkeeper's eyes narrowed, calculating. "Three shillings for the lot."

Mabel's heart sank. The price wouldn't cover half of what she needed for rent. "Sir, the materials alone—"

"Take it or leave it. Times are hard all over."

The coins felt cold in her palm as she stepped back into the bitter wind. Her feet ached from hours of walking, and the sun hung low in the sky. The thought of the long walk home made her legs tremble.

The cottage windows were dark when she finally reached home. Inside, the hearth held only cooling ashes. Emma sat at their mother's bedside, Henry curled against her shoulder, both children dozing.

"Mama's been sleeping since midday," Emma whispered as Mabel hung her coat.

Mabel touched her mother's forehead — still warm with fever. The cupboard yielded only a handful of potatoes and half a loaf of bread. She sliced the portions thin, warming them over the rekindled fire.

"Tell us about the princess again," Henry murmured as they huddled around the table. "The one Papa used to read."

Mabel's eyes watered at the mention of their father, but she forced a smile. "Once there was a princess who lived in a tower made of crystal..." The familiar words flowed as she remembered her father's voice, rich and warm, bringing the story to life. Emma's eyes brightened, and Henry's shoulders relaxed as she described the princess' clever escape using nothing but moonbeams and courage.

The tale couldn't fill their bellies or heal their mother, but for a moment, the cottage felt warmer, touched by an echo of happier days.

WINTER

*S*now fell in thick curtains, transforming Hampstead's familiar streets. Mabel's boots crunched through fresh drifts as she navigated the white-shrouded village. It was her seventeenth birthday, but she barely gave that a thought. She had work to do.

The bundle of lace pressed against her chest, protected beneath her threadbare coat. Each step required careful placement — the snow had buried the usual landmarks she used to guide her path to London.

Her breath clouded before her face, carried away by bitter gusts that cut through her clothing. Her mother's declining health and the children's hungry faces drove her forward despite the biting cold. She paused at the crossroads, squinting through the swirling white. The usual five-mile trek would take longer in these conditions.

The snow muffled all sound except the whisper of falling flakes and the rapid beating of her heart. No one else braved the weather — even the baker's chimney stood cold and dark. Her fingers, red and stiff inside worn gloves, clutched tighter to her precious cargo.

Back at the cottage, Mabel eased open the bedroom door. The fire's glow barely reached the corners where shadows gathered thick as cobwebs. Mary lay still beneath a pile of blankets, her breathing shallow and uneven. Each inhale rattled in her chest like dried leaves.

The strong hands that had once guided Mabel through complex lace patterns now lay limp against the coverlet. Mary's skin held the translucent quality of fine porcelain, blue veins visible beneath. Her dark hair, streaked with silver, fanned across the pillow – no longer secured in its usual neat bun.

Mabel approached on silent feet, not wanting to disturb what little rest her mother found. The familiar scent of lavender that once surrounded Mary had faded, replaced by the sharp tang of illness. She adjusted the blankets with gentle movements, tucking them closer around her mother's shoulders.

THE EVENING SHADOWS crept across Mary's bedchamber, cast by the single candle flickering on the bedside table. Mabel perched on the edge of the bed, Emma and Henry pressed close on either side. Their small hands linked together, forming a chain of warmth in the chill of the room.

Mary's chest rose and fell with effort beneath the patchwork quilt. Her fingers, once nimble with needle and thread, now lay still against the fabric. The silence hung heavy, broken only by the soft pop of the dying fire and Mary's labored breathing.

Emma's grip tightened on Mabel's hand. Henry's shoulders trembled, though he made no sound. They both seemed to understand what Mabel had known for weeks - that their mother's strength was failing like the last rays of sunset.

Her mother's eyes fluttered open, finding Mabel's face in the dim light. Her hand lifted slightly from the coverlet, reaching for her eldest daughter. Mabel caught it gently between her own, feeling the bird-like fragility of her mother's bones beneath paper-thin skin.

"Mabel." Mary's voice emerged as soft as falling snow. She drew a careful breath, each word measured with precious strength. "Promise me... keep them together." Her gaze drifted to Emma and Henry before returning to Mabel's face. "If you can, but keep them safe above all."

Tears blurred Mabel's vision as she nodded, her mother's words settling across her shoulders like a heavy cloak. "I promise, Mama." Her voice caught in her throat, thick with emotion she struggled to contain.

Mary's fingers squeezed weakly against Mabel's palm, the gesture carrying all the love her failing strength could no longer express.

PASSING

$\mathcal{T}$he grey morning light filtered through the threadbare curtains, casting pallid shadows across Mary's face. Mabel knelt beside the bed, her mother's hand clasped between her own. The familiar roughness of Mary's fingers, worn from years of lace-making, felt cooler now.

Emma and Henry huddled near the doorway, their small frames pressed together like frightened birds. The fire had died hours ago, leaving only ash and the lingering scent of burned wood.

Their mother's breath came slower, each rise of her chest more shallow than the last. Mabel traced the delicate bones of her mother's hand, memorising every line and callus. The silence stretched between each laboured breath until, with a soft exhale, Mary's chest stilled.

Mabel's grip tightened on her mother's hand. The quiet pressed against her ears like cotton wool, broken only by Emma's muffled sob from the doorway.

THE COTTAGE WALLS seemed to close in during the days that followed. Emma refused to leave Henry's side, following him from room to room like a shadow. They slept curled together in Emma's narrow bed, their faces tear-stained even in sleep.

Mabel moved through the motions of their daily routine — stoking the fire, preparing thin porridge, attempting to coax food into her siblings. But their mother's absence echoed in every corner. The lace table sat untouched, gathering dust. Their mother's shawl still hung by the door, its familiar pattern a reminder that cut fresh each time Mabel passed.

At night, after tucking Emma and Henry into bed, Mabel would sit at the kitchen table, surrounded by silence. The familiar creaks of the cottage boards seemed hollow now, each sound a reminder of what they'd lost. During the day, Emma's drawings lay abandoned, and Henry's wooden toys remained scattered where they'd fallen, neither child able to find comfort in their usual pastimes.

A sharp knock rattled the cottage door. Mabel lifted her head from the kitchen table, her neck stiff from hours of worrying over their dwindling coins. The knock came again, harder this time.

Mr Thackeray's bulk filled the doorframe, his shadow stretching across the worn floorboards. The landlord's face pinched with distaste as he surveyed the sparse room.

"Miss Fairchild, your rent's three months past due." He pulled a ledger from his coat. "With your mother's passing, I'll be needing that settled."

"Please, sir. We've only just—"

"Business is business." He thumbed through the pages. "Four pounds, seven shillings. You've one month to pay, or out you go."

The amount struck her like a physical blow. Their entire savings wouldn't cover half.

"But where would we—"

"Not my concern." He snapped the ledger shut. "One month."

The door closed with a thud that seemed to echo through Mabel's bones. Emma appeared in the kitchen doorway, Henry clutching her hand.

"Are we going to lose the cottage?" Henry's voice quavered.

Mabel crossed to them, pulling both into her arms though her own heart felt like lead. "We'll find a way." The words tasted hollow on her tongue. "I promise we'll sort something out."

But as she held them, her mind raced through their options. The lace table might fetch a price, though selling it felt like betraying their mother's memory. Her own pieces barely brought in enough for bread. The thought of their father in Maidstone Prison, unable to help, pressed against her chest like iron bands.

Emma's thin shoulders shook beneath Mabel's hands. Henry's face pressed warm and damp against her neck. They were so young, so fragile. And now it all rested on her — their home, their safety, their future.

THE FIRE'S glow cast dancing shadows across the cottage walls as Mabel pulled her mother's wooden box from beneath the bed. Her fingers traced the familiar patterns carved into its surface before lifting the lid. Inside lay her mother's most precious lace pieces, each one folded with careful precision.

Mabel lifted out the wedding tablecloth, its delicate patterns still pristine despite the years. She spread it across her lap, her fingers following the intricate paths her mother's hands had traced. The firelight caught each stitch, transforming the simple thread into something magical.

The cloth in her hands brought back memories of watching her mother work, her skilled fingers weaving stories into every pattern. Each piece held echoes of her mother's voice explaining techniques, sharing secrets passed down through generations.

Emma's sketchbook lay open on the table, filled with half-finished flower drawings. Mabel reached for a fresh page, her charcoal stick hovering over the paper. The design formed slowly beneath her hand — peonies like those in their old garden, intertwined with the forget-me-nots her mother had loved so dearly.

As she sketched, Mabel's tears fell silently onto the page, smudging the careful lines. She wiped them away with her sleeve, refusing to let grief overtake her work. This piece would be different from her usual patterns – not just lace, but a story woven in thread. Her mother's story.

The fire crackled lower as Mabel worked, adding delicate details to the design. Each petal and leaf spoke of her mother's gentle strength, her unwavering love for her children. Through the window, dawn's first light began to creep across the sky, but Mabel barely noticed, lost in the rhythm of creation and memory.

Henry stirred in his sleep from the corner bed, and Emma's quiet breathing reminded Mabel of all she must protect. She looked down at the design taking shape before her — this would be her tribute to her mother, but also her promise to carry forward everything her mother had taught her.

DIRE CIRCUMSTANCES

*M*abel's eyes fluttered open at the first hint of gray light seeping through the cottage windows. Her fingers, stiff from yesterday's work, found the rough strike of a match. The candle's glow cast shadows across the wooden table where scraps of half-finished lace lay scattered like fallen snow.

The flame wavered as she settled onto the hard chair, her mother's old cushion long since sold. Her hands moved of their own accord, weaving patterns she'd watched Mama create countless times. The thread slipped through her raw fingertips, transforming into delicate flowers and vines that would barely fetch enough to feed them for a day.

The familiar five-mile trek to London stretched before her like a sentence. Her feet knew every cobblestone, every muddy patch, every corner where she might find a merchant willing to part with a few pennies for her work. The weight of her lace bundle seemed to grow heavier with each passing day, though she carried less and less to sell.

Emma stirred in the corner bed she shared with Henry, her eyes finding Mabel's in the dim light. The worry etched across her young face cut deeper than any physical pain. Henry's cheeks had grown hollow, his usually bright eyes dulled by hunger. Their empty pantry mocked Mabel's efforts — a single loaf of bread and handful of potatoes wouldn't last another day.

Mabel's shoulders slumped as she counted the meagre coins from yesterday's sales. Three pence wouldn't buy enough to fill their bellies. The faces of her siblings haunted her steps, their trust in her ability to provide a burden heavier than any load of lace she'd ever carried.

Her fingers trembled as she tied off another row of intricate stitches. The pattern blurred before her eyes, exhaustion threatening to overtake her determination. But she couldn't stop. Wouldn't stop. Not while Emma and Henry needed her.

THE CANDLE FLICKERED across three bowls of watery soup, casting long shadows across the cottage table. Mabel's spoon scraped the bottom of her own bowl, the sound harsh in the evening quiet. Emma pushed a lone potato around while Henry stared at his reflection in the broth.

"Emma, Henry." Mabel's voice caught. She set down her spoon. "We need to talk about our situation."

Emma's head snapped up, her fingers tightening around her spoon. Henry's lower lip trembled.

"The money from the lace..." Mabel swallowed hard. "It's not enough anymore. The rent, the food – I've tried everything, but—"

"We could eat less," Emma whispered.

Mabel pulled them both close, their small frames fitting against her sides like they had when Mama read stories by the fire. "No, my loves. You're already too thin." She pressed her cheek against Emma's hair, fighting back tears. "I promise I'm doing everything I can. Everything."

The words tasted like ash in her mouth. Each morning

brought new worries – Emma's dress growing looser, Henry's persistent cough, the landlord's threatening glances. The coins from her lace sales barely covered bread, let alone medicine or warm clothes for the approaching winter.

Emma's once-bright eyes had dulled, the spark of creativity fading as hunger gnawed at their bellies. She no longer sketched flowers in the margins of her paper or hummed while helping with chores. Even Henry's playful spirit dimmed, his wooden soldiers gathering dust in the corner.

Late that night, Mabel sat alone by the dying embers. The moonlight caught the silver threads of her latest piece — hours of work that would fetch pennies at best. Her fingers traced the pattern, but her mind wandered to Mrs Winters at the Hampstead Orphanage. The stern woman's reputation for kindness warred with Mabel's promise to Mama.

The truth settled heavy in her chest: love meant making impossible choices. No matter how many hours she worked or how fine her lace, she couldn't keep them safe and fed on her own. The orphanage might offer what she couldn't – regular meals, warm beds, proper care.

Tears fell onto the lace as Mabel faced what she'd been avoiding for weeks. She would have to break her heart to save theirs.

HAMPSTEAD ORPHANAGE

*D*awn crept through the cottage windows as Mabel folded Emma's threadbare dress into a small bundle. She rubbed her thumb across a patch she'd sewn last spring—the day their mother had taught Emma how to press flowers. The memory stung like salt in an open wound.

"What can I take?" Henry clutched his wooden spinning top, the paint chipped from countless hours of play.

"The top, of course." Mabel's voice cracked. She reached for the small leather-bound book of poetry their father had read to them. "And this. Papa would want you to have it."

Emma stood in the corner, her sketchbook pressed against her chest. Dried flowers peeked from between its pages—their mother's teaching materials for her lace patterns.

"Your drawings will bring colour to—" Mabel couldn't finish the sentence. Instead, she wrapped her mother's shawl around Emma's shoulders, breathing in the lingering scent of lavender.

The cottage felt hollow as they gathered their precious few belongings. Henry's wooden soldiers lined up for one last battle on the windowsill. Emma's pressed flowers decorated the mantle like paper ghosts. Their mother's lace table stood bare, except for the wedding tablecloth Mabel had wrapped carefully in oilcloth. She secured that in her bag.

The path to Hampstead Orphanage stretched before them, grey and endless. Mabel gripped Emma's hand in her right, Henry's in her left. Each step away from the cottage drove splinters into her heart. The wind whipped at their clothes, carrying the scent of approaching rain.

Behind them, their home grew smaller. Mabel glanced back at the climbing roses their mother had planted, now wild and untamed. The window where she'd watched her father grade papers in the evenings. The crooked chimney that had leaked smoke into their warm kitchen.

Emma stumbled, her grip tightening on Mabel's hand. Henry dragged his feet, the book of poetry clutched against his chest. The cottage disappeared around a bend in the road, taking with it the last traces of their mother's laughter, their father's stories, the life they'd known.

The iron gates of Hampstead Orphanage loomed ahead, their black bars casting long shadows across the gravel path. Mabel's heart hammered as she guided Emma and Henry toward the entrance. A tall woman in a grey dress emerged from the doorway — Mrs Winters, the orphanage monitor. Her stern features softened as she took in the three siblings, and something in her eyes reminded Mabel of candlelight through stained glass.

"The Fairchild children." Mrs Winters' voice carried both authority and gentleness. She studied them each in turn, noting Emma's tight grip on her sketchbook and Henry's wooden top peeking from his pocket. Her gaze lingered on their worn clothes and hollow cheeks before settling on Mabel. "You've done right by them, bringing them here. How old?"

"Thirteen and ten. Although Henry's almost eleven."

Mrs Winters nodded, but said nothing more on the matter.

"They'll stay together?" Mabel's voice caught.

"Together." Mrs. Winters nodded. "We maintain strict schedules here — meals at seven, noon, and six. Lessons in the morning, chores in the afternoon. But the children share dormitories by age groups, and siblings are permitted time together during recreation hours."

Mabel knelt before Emma and Henry, the gravel biting through her thin dress. She took their hands in hers, remembering how their mother had held them the same way.

"Listen to me." She squeezed their fingers. "You must be brave now, both of you. Henry, watch over your sister. Emma, keep drawing your beautiful flowers." Her throat tightened. "Promise me you'll look after each other."

"Promise," they whispered in unison.

"This isn't forever." Mabel pulled them close. "Once I find proper work, a real place for us... I'll come back for you both. We'll be together again." She pressed her lips to their foreheads, tasting salt. "Remember that I love you. More than all the stars in the sky."

Through the iron gates, Mabel caught glimpses of children scattered across the orphanage grounds. A group of girls skipped rope near a weathered oak tree, their laughter carrying across the yard like wind chimes. Others sat alone on wooden benches, shoulders hunched, faces turned away from the world. One small boy traced patterns in the dirt with a stick, his eyes fixed on nothing at all.

Her chest tightened as she recognised the same loss in their faces that she'd seen in Emma's mirror that morning. These children had their own stories of separation—mothers claimed by illness, fathers lost to accidents or prison. Some, like Emma and Henry, had known the warmth of a family's love. Others might never have felt a mother's embrace or heard a father's bedtime story.

Mrs Winters guided Emma toward a cluster of girls around her age. One offered Emma a piece of chalk, pointing to hopscotch squares drawn on the flagstones. Henry lingered by the oak tree, his wooden top still clutched in his pocket, watching older boys play marbles in the dust.

The sight of them there — without their mother's gentle guidance or their father's proud smile — carved a hollow space in Mabel's heart. No more evenings around the lace table, learning patterns passed down through generations. No more poetry readings by firelight, their father's voice painting pictures of daffodils and lonely clouds.

But as Emma sketched a flower in the dirt for her new companions, and Henry finally pulled out his top to show a curious boy, Mabel felt a flutter of something lighter than grief. Their mother's strength lived in Emma's artistic touch. Their father's kindness showed in Henry's shy smile. Though separated by iron gates and stone walls, the invisible threads of family bound them still — as delicate and enduring as their mother's finest lace.

Mabel's feet refused as the heavy wooden doors of the orphanage groaned open, and all the children started making their way inside, Emma and Henry in tow.

Emma's sketchbook slipped, scattering dried flowers across the threshold. She dropped to her knees, scrambling to gather them, but a gust of wind carried several away. Mabel watched the delicate petals dance through the air — fragments of their mother's garden taking flight.

Mrs Winters knelt beside Emma, helping her collect the remaining flowers. Her movements were gentle, almost maternal, as she tucked them back between the pages. The sight blurred as tears filled Mabel's eyes.

The doors closed with a hollow thud that echoed through Mabel's bones. Through the warped glass windows, she caught a final glimpse of Emma's brown curls and Henry's threadbare jacket before they vanished into the shadows of the hallway.

Cold air bit at her cheeks. Mabel wrapped her arms around

herself, feeling the outline of her mother's wedding tablecloth beneath her coat.

Her legs trembled as she forced herself to turn away from the orphanage. Each step down the gravel path felt like walking on broken glass. But with every painful stride, determination blazed brighter in her. She would find work — proper work. She would save every penny, create the finest lace London had ever seen. She would build a home worthy of Emma's drawings and Henry's stories.

The iron gates clanged shut behind her. Mabel squared her shoulders against the wind, her mother's strength flowing through her veins like fire. She had promised to keep them safe above all else. Now she would promise herself: this separation would not be forever.

CRACKS

*M*abel grasped the brass door handle of Madame Chantal's Lace Emporium. The polished windows displayed intricate wedding veils and delicate collars that reminded her of her mother's work. Her reflection ghosted across the glass – a pale face framed by escaping wisps of hair she'd tried to tame into respectability.

Inside, a bell announced her presence. The shop smelled of fresh linen and beeswax. Behind the counter, a woman in silk rustled forward, her lips pursing at the sight of Mabel's darned sleeves and scuffed boots.

"We're not purchasing today." The woman's voice cut like scissors through fabric.

"I've come about a position." Mabel lifted her chin. "I'm experienced in Brussels and Honiton techniques—"

"References?"

The word fell between them like a stone. "My mother taught me. She made lace for the finest houses in Hampstead—"

"No references?" The woman's eyebrows arched. "Good day."

The pattern repeated at Watson & Sons, at Mrs Hartley's Notions, at The Royal Lace Company. Each doorway promised possibility, each threshold offered hope. But their eyes saw only her worn clothes, her empty hands where letters of recommendation should be.

"We don't hire vagrants," sniffed the manager at Pembroke's Fine Goods.

"Orphan, are you?" The clerk at Harrison's peered at her through his spectacles. "Probably light-fingered. Can't risk it."

With each rejection, the weight of her father's imprisonment pressed heavier on her shoulders. The shame of it clung to her like cobwebs, invisible but impossible to brush away. They didn't see her skill with a bobbin, her eye for pattern, the years spent learning at her mother's table. They saw only what they feared — a girl with no history they could trust, no name they could verify.

The door's bell jangled behind her with a finality that made Mabel's shoulders cave. Through the glass, she caught fragments of conversation — silk-clad ladies discussing their latest orders, their laughter spilling onto the street like expensive perfume.

"Did you see her dress?" The words drifted out. "As if anyone would trust their fine lace to—"

Mabel's legs carried her away before she could hear more. Each step felt heavier than the last until she found a wrought-iron bench beneath a leafless tree. The metal's chill seeped through her thin dress as she sank down.

Her mother's voice whispered in her memory: "Keep your head high, love. Your hands hold magic in them." But her mother hadn't known how doors would slam, how eyes would slide past as if Mabel were invisible, how her father's good name had transformed into a curse that followed her through London's streets.

She pulled her coat tighter, fingers brushing the oilcloth-wrapped wedding tablecloth inside. The lace within held patterns her mother had created — flowers and vines that had once adorned their cottage table. Now it felt like lead in her pocket, weighing her down with memories of warmth she couldn't recapture.

A gust of wind caught her skirts, carrying the smell of roasting chestnuts from a nearby vendor. Her stomach clenched at the reminder of meals shared around their old table, of Emma's drawings and Henry's laughter. The ache of missing them twisted deeper than hunger.

Mabel pressed her palms against her eyes, fighting back tears that threatened to fall. Her mother's strength had made everything seem possible — even in their darkest hours, Mama had found beauty in the smallest things. But now, faced with closed doors and cold stares, Mabel felt that inherited strength beginning to crack.

Night crept across London's streets like spilled ink. Mabel's legs ached from hours of walking, each step heavier than the last. Shop windows darkened one by one, their warmth and light sealed away behind locked doors. The few coins in her pocket wouldn't secure even the cheapest lodging.

Her boots scraped against cobblestones as she searched for shelter. The stone facade of a Church rose before her, its shadowed doorway offering a pocket of refuge from the wind. Mabel sank down into the alcove, her back pressed against the cold stone. She arranged her few belongings close — the precious wedding tablecloth tucked safely inside her coat, protecting it from the grime of the streets.

Carriages rattled past, their wheels throwing up slush. Voices drifted through the darkness — merchants closing their shops, ladies returning from evening calls, children being hurried home to warm beds. Each sound pierced her thin coat like needles.

"Did you promise them, Emma? Do you promise to mind Henry?" She whispered the words they'd exchanged at the orphanage gates, clinging to the memory of their faces. Her fingers found the rough edge of Emma's last drawing, folded carefully in her pocket. Henry's wooden top had left an impression in the paper where she'd wrapped them together.

Fat snowflakes began to fall, transforming the grimy street into something almost beautiful. The white dusting did nothing to warm Mabel's shoulders or stop the shivers that ran through her frame. Around her, others emerged from shadows – hunched figures seeking doorways and alley corners, each trying to claim some small shelter from the growing cold. A woman clutching a bundle hurried past, her thin shawl pulled tight. Two children huddled together beneath a cart, sharing a ragged blanket.

The stone leached what little warmth remained in Mabel's bones. She tucked her knees closer to her chest, trying to make herself smaller against the chill that crept through every seam of her clothing.

COLLAPSE

*M*abel stirred from her makeshift bed in the church doorway. Her bones ached from the cold stone, but something else pulled at her chest — a heaviness that made each breath catch. She coughed into her sleeve, the sound echoing off the church walls.

The wedding tablecloth remained secure inside her coat, though dampness had seeped into the fabric overnight. Mabel pressed her palm against the stone to steady herself as she rose, her head swimming with the motion.

"Just need to eat something," she whispered, counting the few coins left in her pocket. Perhaps enough for a crust of bread, if she found the right vendor.

The morning crowd filled the streets as Mabel made her way toward the market. Her feet dragged against the cobblestones, each step requiring more effort than the last. The cough returned, deeper this time, but she forced it down. She couldn't afford to show weakness — not when she needed to convince someone to buy her lace.

Stalls lined the narrow lanes, merchants calling out their wares. The press of bodies and mix of smells made Mabel's stomach turn. She stumbled, catching herself against a cart of vegetables. The vendor shot her a suspicious look.

"Sorry," she mumbled, pushing away. The world tilted strangely, buildings seeming to lean inward. Her chest tightened as she tried to draw breath, each inhale shorter than the last.

Sweat beaded on her forehead despite the morning chill. She reached for a wall to steady herself, but her hand met empty air. The crowd swirled around her in a blur of colours and noise. Her legs felt like water, unable to hold her upright.

"Excuse me," she tried to say to a passing woman, but the words came out as barely a whisper. Black spots danced at the edges of her vision. She needed to sit down, just for a moment, just to catch her breath...

The cobblestones rushed up to meet Mabel as her legs crumpled beneath her. She clutched her mother's tablecloth to her chest, her fingers white-knuckled around the precious bundle as she slumped against the cold steps of St Bartholomew's Hospital.

Each breath came in shallow gasps. Fire burned in her lungs, yet her body shook with bone-deep chills. The morning fog swirled around her, or perhaps it was just her vision blurring at the edges.

Boots and skirts swept past, their wearers averting their eyes from another fallen unfortunate on London's streets. A woman pulled her child closer, hurrying past. A gentleman adjusted his hat, quickening his stride. Their indifference cut deeper than the winter wind.

"Miss? Miss, can you hear me?" A voice pierced through the haze. A figure knelt beside her, blocking the weak morning light. "Someone fetch help! This girl needs assistance!"

The stranger's words seemed to come from far away, muffled as though underwater. Mabel tried to focus on the face above her, but her eyes wouldn't cooperate. More voices joined the first, a crowd gathering around her prone form.

Hands lifted her, and Mabel fought to keep hold of her bundle. The world tilted and swayed as they carried her through streets that grew progressively narrower and darker. The air grew thick with the stench of unwashed bodies and despair.

A building loomed before her, its grey walls bleeding into the colourless sky. "Whitechapel Workhouse…" someone whispered to her.

Mabel's head lolled against someone's shoulder as they guided her through dim corridors. Shadows danced on grimy walls, and distant coughs echoed through the halls. Fragments of conversation floated around her:

"…no room in the hospital…"

"…another one for the women's ward…"

"…fever, most likely…"

The voices faded in and out as they led her deeper into the building's depths, toward rows of iron beds where others lay moaning.

THE WORKHOUSE

*M*abel's eyes fluttered open to darkness broken only by thin shafts of grey light filtering through high windows. The straw mat beneath her crackled as she shifted, sending wisps of musty air into her face. Her chest still ached, but the crushing weight had lifted enough to breathe.

Rows of iron beds stretched into shadows, each holding a hunched form or prostrate figure. The air hung thick with the mingled scents of unwashed bodies, medicine, and something else — a heavy despair that seemed to seep from the very walls.

A woman in the next bed stared at the ceiling, her sunken eyes reflecting nothing. Another huddled beneath a thin blanket, shoulders shaking with silent sobs. Across the aisle, skeletal fingers plucked at threadbare sheets while cracked lips moved in soundless prayer.

Mabel's hand flew to her chest, relief flooding through her as she felt the familiar bundle of her mother's tablecloth still secured beneath her dress. The touch of the fabric anchored her to who she was, even as the workhouse threatened to strip away her identity.

A cough echoed from somewhere in the gloom, followed by another, then another — a symphony of suffering that bounced off stone walls and iron bed frames. Some faces turned toward the sound, while others remained fixed in vacant stares, as though they'd forgotten how to respond to the world around them.

"Water?" croaked a voice nearby. Mabel turned to see a young woman, perhaps her own age, reaching toward her with trembling fingers. But no one came. No one answered. The hand fell back to the bed, and the woman's eyes closed in resignation.

Mabel's throat tightened as she surveyed the room again. These were not just bodies in beds — they were stories interrupted, lives derailed by circumstance or misfortune. Like her. The realisation settled over her like a physical weight: she was now one of them, another soul caught in this web of poverty and illness.

MABEL'S FINGERS trembled as she pulled at loose threads from her dress hem. The coarse fabric resisted, but she persisted, gathering strands one by one. Her chest still burned with each breath, yet the familiar motions of preparing thread brought comfort amid the workhouse's bleakness.

She'd seen how quickly spirits broke here. The vacant stares, the slumped shoulders, the whispered prayers that grew fainter each day. But her mother's voice echoed in her memory: "Our hands create beauty even in darkness."

The threads were nothing like the fine materials she'd once worked with. These were rough, uneven, pulled from clothing already worn thin. Still, her fingers remembered the patterns, weaving simple flowers and leaves. The work steadied her racing thoughts, kept her mind from dwelling on Emma and Henry's faces at the orphanage gates.

Between fits of coughing, she worked. The piece grew slowly – small, imperfect, but alive with meaning. Other women watched from their beds, some inching closer to see the emerging design.

"It's like sunlight," whispered the young woman who'd asked for water. Mabel finished the piece — a small square with a simple flower pattern – and pressed it into her trembling hands.

As strength returned to her limbs, the workhouse masters put her to work scrubbing floors and washing linens. The endless hours bent over stone floors left her back aching, her knees raw against the rough surface. Her hands cracked and bled from the harsh lye soap, but each night she gathered more threads from fraying sheets and discarded clothing. Hidden away in her thin bed, she wove them into tiny tokens — a leaf edged with morning dew, a star burning bright against darkness, a bird in flight seeking freedom beyond the workhouse walls.

She gave these to women who'd lost hope: the mother separated from her children, the widow whose hands shook too badly to work, the girl who'd stopped speaking entirely. Some tucked them into pockets or pinned them inside collars – small reminders that beauty could exist even here.

"Teach me?" asked an elderly woman one evening, her gnarled fingers reaching for Mabel's latest piece. Soon a small circle formed in the shadows after work hours. Mabel showed them basic stitches, watching their faces soften as they created something of their own.

A STRANGER'S KINDNESS

hrough the haze of a light fever and fatigue, Mabel's fingers moved in familiar patterns. A scrap of thread pulled from her dress became wings, then a beak, then finally the suggestion of a sparrow taking flight. The stitches were tiny, almost invisible against the rough cloth, but they captured something of freedom.

The workhouse door creaked open. Mabel tucked her work beneath the thin blanket, but not before catching a glimpse of a well-dressed woman stepping into the ward. Her silk skirts rustled against the stone floor as she moved between the rows of beds, distributing parcels wrapped in brown paper.

"Mrs Bartlett's come with donations," whispered the woman in the next bed. "Always brings good bread, she does. Clergyman's wife."

Mabel watched as Mrs Bartlett paused at each bed, offering not just packages but gentle words. Her face carried none of the pinched disapproval Mabel had grown used to seeing from charitable visitors. Instead, warmth radiated from her eyes as she spoke with each woman.

When Mrs Bartlett reached Mabel's bed, a stray beam of

sunlight caught the thread work peeking out from beneath the blanket. Mrs Bartlett's hand stilled mid-motion as she was about to pass over a package.

"What's this?" She lifted the corner of the blanket. The sparrow seemed to quiver in the light, its wings caught mid-beat against the coarse fabric. "Did you create this?"

Mabel nodded, uncertain whether to expect praise or punishment for using workhouse materials.

Mrs Bartlett inspected the delicate stitches. "Such fine work, and with so little to work with." She glanced at Mabel's face, then back to the embroidery. "This isn't just stitching — there's artistry here. Real skill."

Mabel's smile emerged tentative and small, like a flower pushing through frost. Her fingers brushed the tiny sparrow she'd created. "My mother taught me. We made lace together, proper Brussels and Honiton pieces." The memory of her mother's patient hands guiding her own made her voice catch. "Even when we had nothing else, we could create something beautiful."

Mrs Bartlett settled on the edge of the bed, her silk skirts pooling against the rough blanket. She didn't flinch from the dirt or despair that clung to everything in the workhouse. Instead, she leaned closer, examining the intricate work with genuine interest.

"Tell me more about your lace," Mrs Bartlett's voice carried the warmth of summer gardens. "These stitches speak of years of practice."

The words spilled from Mabel like water from a spring. She described the peony patterns her mother favoured, the delicate forget-me-nots she'd woven into wedding veils, the countless hours spent perfecting each stitch until her fingers bled.

"But how long have you been here for, my dear?" Mrs Bartlett asked gently.

"I'm... I'm not sure. Six months maybe? Maybe more." Mabel shrugged in apology.

Mrs Bartlett touched Mabel's hand, her grip firm and reassuring. "You mustn't let this gift wither here. The world needs beauty, especially in its darkest corners." She reached into her reticule and withdrew a small packet of thread. "Here. Create something magnificent."

"But I couldn't possibly—"

"You can and you will." Mrs Bartlett's eyes crinkled with kindness. "I know several ladies who commission fine lace work. They appreciate true artistry when they see it." She patted Mabel's hand. "Keep working. I'll speak of your talents in the right circles."

DETERMINATION

*N*ight settled over the workhouse like a heavy blanket, bringing with it the chorus of coughs and quiet sobs that echoed through the women's ward. Mabel's fingers trembled as she clutched her mother's wedding table-cloth beneath her thin dress, and she thought of Mrs Bartlett's kindness earlier that day.

Emma's face floated before her closed eyes — the way her sister's hands moved when she drew flowers, the light in her eyes when she discovered a new bloom. The sound of Henry's laugh echoed in what now felt like a distant memory.

The rough blanket scratched against Mabel's skin as she curled onto her side, fighting another wave of chills. Around her, women moaned in their sleep, their dreams haunted by the same desperation that filled their waking hours. The thread Mrs Bartlett had given her lay carefully wrapped in a scrap of cloth under her pillow, but Mabel's hands shook too much to work with it now.

She pressed her face into the thin pillow, breathing in the musty scent of straw and illness. The promise she'd made at the orphanage gates echoed in her mind: "I'll come back for you both. We'll be together again." The words felt hollow in this place of shadow and suffering, yet Mabel clung to them like a lifeline.

In the darkness, she traced the familiar patterns of her mother's lace with trembling fingers. Each loop and swirl told a story of love, of family, of moments shared around their cottage table. The delicate threads had survived poverty, grief, and now the workhouse — just as Mabel must survive.

She wouldn't let this place claim her. Emma and Henry needed her. Somewhere beyond these walls lay a future where her art could feed them, clothe them, and bring them home. Mabel's hands steadied as she gripped the tablecloth tighter, determination rising.

THREE DAYS PASSED in the workhouse's dim confines before Mrs Bartlett's return cast a ray of light through the gloom. Her silk skirts rustled against the wooden floor as she approached Mabel's cot, her face bright with purpose.

"My dear, I've spoken about your work to several acquaintances." Mrs Bartlett said. "There's a position available at Finch's Lace Shop in Cheapside. The owner seeks skilled hands for their workshop."

Mabel's heart skipped. Her fingers, still raw from pulling threads, twisted in the blanket. "A position? At Finch's?"

"Indeed. I've arranged an interview for you tomorrow morning." Mrs. Bartlett's eyes crinkled with warmth. "Mr Finch was quite interested when I described your mastery of the Brussels technique."

The word 'tomorrow' echoed in Mabel's ears. She pushed herself to sit straighter, ignoring the lingering weakness in her limbs. "I... I don't know how to thank you."

"Your talent deserves recognition, child." Mrs Bartlett

touched Mabel's arm. "The pay isn't grand, but it includes lodging. Far better than..." Her gaze swept across the ward's grimy walls.

Hope bloomed in Mabel's chest — fragile as the first spring flower pushing through frost. A real position, with wages and a roof. Perhaps even enough to begin saving for Emma and Henry's care.

"The work will be demanding," Mrs Bartlett continued, smoothing her skirts. "But I've seen your spirit. You have the strength for it, Mabel."

Tears pricked at Mabel's eyes. She blinked them back, unwilling to show weakness when fortune had finally smiled upon her.

FINCH'S LACE SHOP

awn painted Cheapside's buildings in shades of gray as Mabel approached Finch's Lace Shop. The brass bell above the door chimed as she entered, and the scent of cotton and linen wrapped around her like a familiar embrace.

Rows of women hunched over their workstations, fingers dancing across delicate patterns. Light filtered through grimy windows, catching the dust motes that swirled above intricate pieces of Valenciennes and Brussels lace. The careful click of bobbins and whispered counting of stitches filled the air.

A piece of Chantilly lace caught her eye. The creator's hands moved with practiced grace, weaving thread into art.

The floorboards creaked behind her. "You're the one Mrs Bartlett sent?"

Mabel turned. Mr Finch filled the doorway to his office, his waistcoat straining against his belly. His small eyes darted over her worn dress and thin frame.

"Yes, sir." Mabel straightened her spine, willing strength into her voice. "I specialise in the Brussels technique."

He grunted, checking his pocket watch. "Show me your hands."

She held them out, palms up. Despite the workhouse's toll, her fingers remained nimble, marked with the calluses of her craft.

"At least they're clean." He glanced at the workers, who had barely looked up. "Fourteen hours daily, sixpence per week, and a place to sleep which comes your pay . Your bills come out of your wages. No days off unless you're dying." His lips twisted. "And even then, you'd better have a note from a doctor."

Mabel's heart sank at his harsh tone, but she thought of Emma and Henry. Of the orphanage's cold walls. Of her promise. "Yes, sir. When may I start?"

MABEL FOLLOWED Mr Finch down creaking wooden stairs into the shop's basement. The musty air hit her throat, stirring memories of the workhouse she'd fought so hard to escape. Oil lamps cast weak circles of light across the workspace, their flames dancing against damp stone walls.

Her assigned station sat wedged between two other workers — thin women with hollow cheeks who didn't look up as she settled onto the hard wooden stool. The table surface bore deep grooves from years of needlework, and dark patches of water stains spread across the ceiling above.

"Get started on these orders." Mr Finch dropped a stack of patterns beside her. "Mind you don't waste thread."

The hours crawled by like wounded animals. Mabel's fingers, still weak from illness, trembled as she worked the delicate Brussels patterns. The damp air made her bones ache, seeping through her dress despite the August heat above ground.

Her shoulders burned from hunching over the intricate work. The oil lamp's dim light forced her to strain her eyes, and she blinked away tears of exhaustion as the day wore on.

Around her, the other women's breathing mixed with the constant click of bobbins and pins.

A bell chimed somewhere above, marking another hour. Mabel's hands shook as she counted the remaining time until her first shift would end. The wooden stool had long since turned to stone beneath her, and her back screamed in protest at the smallest movement. Still, she forced her fingers to keep weaving, thinking of Emma's smile and Henry's laugh. She could endure this. She had to.

The damp air grew thicker as evening approached, carrying the musty scent of aging fabric and unwashed bodies. Mabel's throat tightened against the familiar workhouse smell, but she focused on her lace, on each careful stitch that brought her closer to reuniting with her siblings.

When the last lamp dimmed, Mabel unrolled her thin pallet beside the work table. The rough fabric scratched against her palms as she smoothed it across the stone floor. Her muscles protested as she lowered herself onto the makeshift bed, the cold seeping through the thin barrier.

She curled onto her side, knees drawn up to fit in the narrow space between table legs. The wooden edge cast a shadow across her face, and she traced the worn grooves with her fingertips, wondering how many others had slept in this same spot, dreaming of escape.

Around her, other women settled onto their own pallets. The rustle of fabric and soft sighs filled the basement. Someone coughed, the sound echoing off stone walls. Another hummed a quiet tune, perhaps to ward off the darkness.

"First night's the hardest," whispered a voice from nearby. "Gets easier when your body learns not to feel."

Mabel shifted, seeking a position that wouldn't press against her bruised hip. The floor's hardness had already left its mark from hours of sitting at the work table. Now it seemed determined to remind her of every bone in her body.

A quiet conversation drifted from the far corner, words too low to make out but carrying the shared exhaustion. Someone else murmured a prayer. The familiar ritual brought memories of Emma's bedtime stories, of Henry's sleepy questions about God.

The basement's damp air wrapped around her like a shroud. Despite the August heat above, cold seeped through the stones. Mabel pulled her shawl tighter, trying to ignore how the other women's whispers reminded her of the workhouse – that same desperate attempt to find comfort in shared suffering.

She closed her eyes, but sleep proved elusive. Her fingers still moved in phantom patterns, weaving invisible lace in the darkness. The day's work had left them raw, each tip tender from countless pin pricks. Yet even this discomfort felt like progress — each stitch brought her closer to saving enough for Emma and Henry's care.

BEAUTY

$\mathcal{T}$he next day, as weak sunlight filtered through the basement's grimy windows, an older woman with silver-streaked hair caught Mabel's eye. She gestured to the empty space beside her on a wooden crate.

"Come share my bread, child. You look ready to faint."

Mabel's legs wobbled as she crossed the room. The woman broke her small loaf in half, pressing a piece into Mabel's hand.

"I'm Agnes." Her weathered fingers showed decades of needlework, but her eyes held a warm gleam. "Twenty years at this table has taught me a thing or two about surviving down here."

Mabel took a careful bite, savouring the simple sustenance. "The patterns blur after hours."

"Ah, that's where most girls go wrong. You must find your rhythm." Agnes demonstrated with her hands, moving as if working invisible bobbins. "Let the lace breathe between stitches. Your mother taught you well — I can see it in your technique."

The mention of her mother made Mabel's throat tighten. Agnes touched her arm gently.

"Look here." She pulled out a scrap of lace from her pocket. "Made this during my breaks. Sometimes we must create beauty for ourselves, not just for Mr Finch's customers."

The delicate pattern showed tiny birds in flight. Mabel traced them with her finger, remembering the sparrows that used to visit their cottage window.

"We all carry stories in our stitches," Agnes said. "That's what keeps the art alive."

A quiet laugh escaped Mabel's lips as Agnes mimicked Mr Finch's perpetual scowl. Other women glanced their way, sharing knowing smiles. For a moment, the basement felt warmer, filled with silent understanding between those who turned thread into dreams.

Mabel returned to her workstation. Her fingers found the bobbins with renewed purpose, weaving patterns that flowed from deep within her memories. The rhythm Agnes spoke of emerged naturally — like her mother's hands guiding her own across the years.

A peony bloomed beneath her touch, each petal more delicate than the last. The other women paused their work, drawn to the intricate dance of her bobbins. Even Sarah, known for her precise Valenciennes edges, leaned closer to study Mabel's technique.

"Look how she turns the corner there," Sarah whispered. "Never seen it done quite like that."

The praise strengthened Mabel's resolve. She incorporated subtle details into each design — tiny forget-me-nots hidden among larger blooms, delicate vines that seemed to catch morning light. These weren't just patterns Mr Finch demanded — they were pieces of her heart, woven into existence.

Emma's face appeared in her mind, bent over her sketchbook filled with flower drawings. Henry's wooden top spun in her memory, its circles reminiscent of the spirals she now crafted in lace. Each stitch brought them closer, each completed piece added to the small pile of coins she tucked away.

Mabel's fingers moved faster, more assured. The basement's damp chill faded as she worked, replaced by the warmth of purpose. This was more than survival — it was her path back to them. She pictured Emma's drawings transformed into lace patterns, Henry's clever hands learning to craft the wooden bobbins they used. Their future home filled with light and the gentle click of bobbins, far from these grim basement walls.

Her current piece took shape — a garden of roses surrounded by delicate butterflies. The other women's whispers grew more frequent, their admiration evident in stolen glances at her work. But Mabel barely noticed, lost in the world she created with thread and skill, each pattern a promise to her siblings that she would find her way back to them.

OUR LITTLE ARTIST

$\mathcal{D}$ays melted together in the basement's dim confines. Mabel's fingers moved mechanically across the lace as moisture crept through her worn shoes and up her skirts. The weak light from the grimy windows played tricks, forcing her to squint until her head ached. Each evening left her bones weary, her hands cramped into painful claws.

She counted her meagre earnings in the dark, calculating how long until she could visit Emma and Henry. The coins felt cold against her palm — not enough, never enough. The shadow of the workhouse loomed in her thoughts, a reminder of what awaited if she failed.

The conditions in Finch's shop were only marginally better than the workhouse, but it meant she had at last fully kicked out the fever that had clung to her chest for what must have been the better part of a year. She no longer felt ill, but still felt endlessly exhausted.

On her pallet at night, Mabel traced the familiar patterns of her mother's tablecloth hidden beneath her thin blanket. Her mother's voice echoed in her memory: "The thread must flow like water, dear one. Let it tell its story."

Her mother's hands had always moved with such grace, even when consumption had stolen her strength. Mabel's own fingers felt clumsy in comparison, though Agnes insisted otherwise.

Sleep came fitfully. The damp air carried whispers of her mother's lessons – about patience, about finding beauty in the smallest details. But it also carried memories of Mama's final days, of promises made and the crushing responsibility that followed.

Mabel shifted on the hard pallet, her shoulders aching from hunching over her work. Other girls whimpered in their sleep nearby, each carrying their own burdens. She closed her eyes and saw her mother's face, remembered the pride in her Mama's expression when Mabel mastered a particularly difficult stitch.

"Your hands were meant for this work," Mama had said. Now those same hands trembled with exhaustion each night, struggling to uphold her mother's artistry while fighting against the desperate circumstances that threatened to drag her back into destitution.

A gentle tap at the basement door broke through the endless rhythm of needlework. Mrs Bartlett's silhouette appeared at the top of the stairs, her presence warming the dank space like sunlight through clouds.

"Just checking on our little artist," Mrs. Bartlett crossed the room, placing a small paper-wrapped package beside Mabel's work station. The scent of candied violets wafted up – the kind her mother once bought for special occasions.

"The church ladies asked after your sparrow design." Mrs Bartlett's eyes crinkled at the corners. "Such delicate work, dear. Your mother taught you well."

The words pierced Mabel's heart. She traced her finger along the stitches of her current piece, a collar adorned with tiny forget-me-nots. Each bloom contained a whispered prayer for Emma and Henry.

"Thank you for your kindness." Mabel's voice caught. The basement's chill seemed to retreat whenever Mrs Bartlett visited, bringing fragments of the world beyond these walls.

After Mrs Bartlett departed, Mabel's hands moved with renewed purpose. Her needle danced through the intricate pattern she'd been developing in secret — one that combined her mother's traditional techniques with her own innovations. Each stitch carried her closer to her dream: a shop of her own, filled with light and beauty, where women could work with dignity.

She pictured herself teaching others, just as her mother had taught her. The basement's gloom transformed in her mind's eye into a bright workroom where creativity flourished. She would create pieces that told stories through their patterns that celebrated life's precious moments rather than simply adorning wealthy women's collars.

The sweet taste of the candied violet lingered on her tongue as she worked, its flavour a reminder that beauty could survive even in the harshest circumstances. Like the delicate flowers preserved in sugar, her mother's legacy would endure through her hands.

ANOTHER'S POCKETS

*M*ist crept under the shop door, as Mabel arranged the day's pieces in the window display, her fingers working quickly to smooth any wrinkles from the delicate patterns. It had taken four months of relentless work downstairs before Mabel was allowed anywhere near the front of the shop, but her skills with lace was undeniable, and Mr Finch had begrudgingly ordered her to aid in the displays.

The weak morning light barely penetrated the grimy glass, but she positioned each item to catch what illumination she could.

The shop bell's sharp ring cut through the quiet. The door swung open with such force that the displays trembled. A domineering lady swept in, her silk skirts rustling against the wooden floor. The lady's presence filled the small space, pushing everything else into shadow.

Mabel's hands stilled on the lace. She watched through the display as the lady's gaze swept across the shop, her lips pursing as though she'd tasted something bitter. The lady's gloved fingers traced along a shelf of boxed lace, leaving pristine tracks in the dust.

"Mr Finch." The lady's voice cracked like a whip. "I require your finest Brussels lace for my daughter Cecilia's coming-out gown."

"Of course, Lady Rowena." Mr Finch scrambled forward, pulling boxes from shelves. His hands shook as he presented piece after piece, but Lady Rowena dismissed each with a flick of her wrist.

"This is barely suitable for a maid's apron." Lady Rowena held up a length of Valenciennes lace. "Surely you have something worthy of the Houghton name?"

More boxes appeared. More dismissals followed. The pile of rejected lace grew as Lady Rowena's patience dwindled.

Mabel straightened, her spine stiffening as she sensed the mounting tension. She adjusted her worn apron, suddenly conscious of every frayed thread and patch. The lady's presence made the shop feel smaller, darker, as though all the air had been drawn toward her commanding figure.

Mabel's fingers brushed against something familiar tangled up in the lace she was laying out. Her heart stopped. The collar she'd been working on in secret had tangled with her work supplies. The delicate piece caught the dim morning light, its intricate pattern of woven flowers and vines visible even in the shop's gloom.

Lady Rowena paused at the door, her sharp gaze falling on the collar. "What's that?"

Mabel's throat tightened as she lifted the piece. The pattern flowed like water, each stitch placed with precision learned at her mother's table. Tiny forget-me-nots bloomed along the edge, while delicate ivy leaves curled through the design.

"This is..." Lady Rowena snatched the collar from Mabel's trembling hands. "This is extraordinary work."

Mr Finch pushed forward, his face reddening. "Ah yes, my daughter's latest piece—"

"Three guineas." Lady Rowena's eyes never left the collar. "I'll take it now."

Mabel's chest tightened. Three guineas — enough for a month's visits to Emma and Henry, with money left for proper food. Words rose in her throat, but fear of losing her position kept them trapped behind her teeth.

The money changed hands, Mr Finch's fingers closing around the coins before Mabel could speak. Lady Rowena tucked the collar into her reticule with surprising gentleness.

"The craftsmanship reminds me of Mary Fairchild's work." Lady Rowena's gaze swept over Mabel. "Such a shame about that family."

Mabel's hands clenched in her apron. Blood rushed in her ears as Lady Rowena turned back to Mr Finch, discussing delivery of additional pieces.

The shop door clicked shut behind Lady Rowena. Mabel watched, frozen, as Mr Finch's fingers closed around the coins, dropping them one by one into his waistcoat pocket. The metallic clink of each guinea struck her like a physical blow.

Her collar — the piece she'd poured her heart into during stolen moments between tasks, threading her mother's techniques into every stitch — had vanished into Lady Rowena's reticule. The payment that could have meant proper meals for Emma and Henry disappeared just as swiftly into Mr Finch's pocket.

Heat rose in Mabel's chest, spreading up her neck. Her fingers curled into her palms until her nails bit flesh. The injustice of it burned — not just the theft of her work, but the casual way Mr Finch had claimed it as his daughter's. As though her hours of labor meant nothing. As though she were nothing more than another tool in his shop, like the needles and thread he provided.

She pressed her lips together, fighting back words that would surely cost her her position. Her hands trembled as she reached for the next piece of lace to arrange, the delicate fabric blurring before her eyes. The basement workroom suddenly felt more confining than ever — a prison where her art served only to line another's pockets.

A single tear splashed onto the lace between her fingers. Mabel quickly wiped it away, grateful that Mr Finch had turned his attention to counting the morning's earnings. The memory of her mother's gentle hands guiding her through complex patterns rose unbidden. How far she'd fallen from those days of creating beauty for beauty's sake, when each piece bore the dignity of their craft rather than the stamp of commerce.

A HANDSOME COLLISION

*T*he bell above the door chimed again, pulling Mabel from her dark thoughts. A young man stood in the doorway, medical texts balanced precariously in his arms. Sunlight caught his dark hair, highlighting threads of auburn. His gray eyes held a gentle intelligence as they swept the cramped shop interior.

"Pardon me," he said, his voice warm and cultured. "I'm looking for some lace pieces. For the women's hospital fundraiser."

The earnestness in his tone caught Mabel's attention. He shifted the books, revealing a well-tailored coat that spoke of wealth, yet his manner lacked the usual condescension she'd grown accustomed to from such customers.

Mr Finch remained absorbed in his ledger, muttering numbers under his breath. Mabel glanced at the young man again, noting how his thoughtful expression reminded her of her father when he'd been deep in lesson planning.

She hurried forward to open the door wider, not wanting him to struggle with his burden. At the same moment, he stepped further into the shop, his attention on the lace displays.

Their bodies collided. The stack of books crashed to the floor, pages fluttering like startled birds. Medical diagrams and scientific texts scattered across the worn floorboards, some sliding beneath display cases.

"Oh!" Mabel dropped to her knees, cheeks burning. "I'm so sorry, sir."

Mabel gathered the scattered papers with trembling fingers, her heart racing at the mess she'd caused. The young man knelt beside her, his movements quick but careful as he collected his medical texts.

"Please, let me help." Their hands met over a diagram of the human heart, and Mabel's breath caught. His fingers were warm against hers, steady and gentle. A strange spark passed between them, making her pause mid-reach.

He laughed — not unkindly — and the sound lifted something in her she thought had died with her mother. "No harm done," he said, stacking the books with practiced ease. "Though I dare say my anatomy texts are getting more exercise than my patients."

Mabel found herself smiling despite her mortification. His eyes crinkled at the corners when he grinned, reminding her of summer afternoons reading with Papa.

"Thank you for your help, Miss..." He trailed off, waiting.

Heat bloomed in her cheeks as she handed him the last book, their fingers brushing again. The shop's dim interior seemed to fade away, leaving only the warmth of his gaze and the flutter of her pulse.

"Miss... I'm Mabel."

The young man smiled. "I'm Edward. Might I purchase this handkerchief?" He selected one from the display, his eyes lingering on her face. "Your lacework is exceptional."

Mr Finch stepped forward to complete the sale, and the spell broke. Edward tucked his purchase away and gathered his books, nodding farewell.

Mabel watched him leave, her heart sinking as she spotted a leather-bound journal beneath the counter. Its pages bristled with handwritten notes — clearly his, left behind in their collision.

Mabel's fingers closed around the leather journal, her heart racing. Edward's careful script filled the pages with medical notes and sketches. She turned toward the door, ready to chase after him.

"Get back to work." Mr Finch's voice cracked like a whip. "That young gentleman is far above your station. Mind your place."

The journal's spine pressed into her palm as her grip tightened. Through the grimy window, she caught a glimpse of Edward's coat disappearing into the morning fog. Her chest ached with the sting of another lost connection, another door closing before she could reach it.

She stood rooted between the counter and the door, the journal heavy in her hands. Mr Finch's dismissive grunt as he returned to his ledger made her cheeks burn. The same fury that had risen when he claimed her collar as his daughter's work bubbled up again.

Edward's figure grew smaller through the clouded glass. His gentle manner and kind eyes had sparked something in her — a reminder of the dignity her family once held, of conversations about poetry and art around their dinner table. Now he vanished into the London streets, taking that brief warmth with him.

She pressed the journal close to her chest, breathing in the leather scent that brought back memories of her father's books. In the dim light of the shop, surrounded by the fruits of her labor that others claimed as their own, Mabel felt a familiar resolve harden in her heart. The same determination that had driven her through five-mile walks in winter, through nights of endless stitching, through saying goodbye to Emma and Henry – it rose again now.

Mr Finch could claim her work, Lady Rowena could dismiss her family's name, but they couldn't take her skill. They couldn't take the artistry flowing through her fingers or the dreams of a better life she held close.

TRAPPED

The first whispers reached Mabel's ears on Tuesday morning. Agnes hunched closer to Sarah near the window, their voices dropping low between the click of needles.

"Three dead two streets over." Agnes' fingers trembled over her work. "Doctor said it was the water."

Mabel's hands stilled on her lace. The basement air pressed heavy against her skin, thick with moisture that beaded on the walls. A drop fell from the ceiling, landing on her collar piece.

By Thursday, more workers huddled in corners, sharing scraps of news between stitches. Mary Beth hadn't come in for two days. Neither had Charlotte. The empty spaces at their workstations gaped like missing teeth.

"A whole family gone in Cheapside." Sarah's voice cracked. "Just like that."

Mabel's stomach clenched as she glanced at the bucket they all shared for drinking water. Dark spots bloomed on its wooden sides, the surface gleaming with the same dampness that coated everything in the basement.

The drip from the ceiling grew worse as rain pattered above. Each splash echoed through the room, mixing with the sound of laboured breathing and muffled coughs. The workers pressed handkerchiefs to their faces, eyes darting between each other at every new sound.

Mabel's fingers found the rough edge of Edward's journal, hidden beneath her workstation. The leather had grown soft with the damp, its pages warping. Her throat tightened as she remembered his kind eyes, his medical books scattered across the floor. What would he say about these conditions? About the water that tasted of metal and earth?

A rat scurried along the wall, its wet fur gleaming in the dim light. The knot in Mabel's stomach twisted tighter. She'd seen enough illness in the workhouse to recognise the signs of coming disaster. The air itself seemed to hold its breath, waiting.

The next morning, footsteps thundered down the basement stairs. Mr Finch burst through the doorway, his face flushed and collar askew. The workers' heads snapped up from their stations as he paced the length of the room, counting under his breath.

"One, two, three..." His finger jabbed the air with each number. "Seven, eight, nine... good."

The iron key scraped in the lock. The sound shot through Mabel's chest like a bolt of lightning.

"Mr Finch?" Agnes rose from her chair. "What's happening?"

"Merely a precaution." He smoothed his waistcoat, but his hands shook. "Cholera's been confirmed on Threadneedle Street. Can't risk it spreading to my establishment."

Sarah pressed her handkerchief to her mouth. "You're locking us in?"

"For everyone's safety." Mr Finch backed toward the stairs. "Continue your work. I'll bring food and water later."

The door slammed shut. The lock turned again.

Mabel's fingers clutched the edge of her workstation as panic clawed up her throat. The basement walls pressed closer, the ceiling lower. She thought of the rat paths along the walls, the dripping water, the shared bucket. They weren't being protected — they were being contained.

Agnes slumped in her chair, her face ashen. "He's left us to die."

The other workers huddled together, whispering prayers and clutching each other's hands. Mabel's mind raced to Emma and Henry, safe at the orphanage. At least they weren't here, trapped in this damp tomb with no way out.

SALVATION

*T*hree days passed in the basement's dim confines. The air grew thick with fear and the sour tang of illness. Mabel watched as Sarah's cough deepened, while Agnes pressed herself against the dampest corner, shivering despite the summer heat. The workers drew closer together, sharing what little comfort remained between them.

"My mother always said to keep the feet warm." Agnes pulled her shawl tighter. "But everything here seeps cold."

Mabel's hands worked mechanically at her lace, mind drifting to Emma's bright sketches, Henry's wooden top. The orphanage stood on high ground, away from the contaminated wells. Mrs Winters would keep them safe. She had to believe that.

Sarah stumbled to the water bucket, her face pale. "The water tastes wrong."

"Don't drink it." Mabel pushed the bucket away. "We can't trust it anymore."

The workers huddled closer as evening approached, their breathing echoing off the damp walls. Young Lucy, barely fourteen, pressed against Martha's side, both girls' faces flushed with fever.

"I feel strange," Lucy whispered. Her fingers fumbled with her thread work.

Martha swayed in her chair. "The room's spinning."

Before Mabel could reach them, both girls crumpled to the floor. Lucy's body twisted with cramping pain while Martha's breath came in sharp gasps.

"Help them!" Agnes cried. The workers crowded around, their faces masks of terror.

Mabel knelt beside the girls, her mother's voice echoing in her memory. Keep them still. Cool their foreheads. But as Lucy's skin burned beneath her touch and Martha's lips turned blue, Mabel's heart hammered. This was beyond any healing her mother had taught her.

"We need a doctor," Mabel's voice cracked. "We need help."

But the locked door stood silent, and Mr Finch was long gone, leaving them to face the disease alone.

A sharp rap echoed through the basement. "Hello? Is anyone there? I'm Edward Montague. I believe I left my journal here a couple days ago."

Mabel's heart leaped at the familiar voice. She pressed against the door. "Mr Montague? Please help us — Mr Finch locked us in. There's cholera, and two girls are very ill."

"Cholera?" Edward's tone shifted. "How many of you are down there?"

"Nine workers. Lucy and Martha collapsed just now. They're burning with fever."

The door handle rattled. "Stand back from the door," Edward commanded. "I need to get you out."

Mabel herded the others away as thuds shook the heavy wood. Edward's shoulder slammed against it once, twice — the frame splintered on the third impact. The door burst inward, revealing Edward's determined face, his medical bag clutched in one hand.

"We need to move quickly." He strode to where Lucy and Martha lay. "These girls require immediate care." His fingers pressed against Lucy's wrist, checking her pulse. "Help me get them stable for transport."

Mabel knelt beside him, supporting Martha's head as Edward assessed her condition. His presence transformed the basement's panic into focused urgency. The other workers gathered around, their faces drawn but ready to help.

"You two" Edward said whilst motioning to Agnes and Sarah, "Can you please find clean cloths, anything we can use for carrying them." His voice remained steady as he worked. "The rest of you, gather your belongings. We need to evacuate this space immediately."

Mabel watched his sure movements as he tended to the girls, his earlier genteel manner replaced by medical authority. His hands moved with practiced efficiency, checking symptoms and preparing the girls for movement. This was a different Edward than the one who'd dropped his books — every gesture spoke of training and purpose.

Through the dim light of dusk, Mabel helped Edward arrange Lucy and Martha onto makeshift stretchers crafted from wooden planks and torn fabric.

"We'll need four people to carry them," Edward directed, his voice firm but gentle. "The hospital's three streets away. Can anyone here manage the weight?"

Agnes and Sarah stepped forward, joined by two other workers. Mabel watched Edward guide them, showing where to grip the stretchers, how to keep the girls level. His hands moved with practiced ease, checking pulses between instructions.

"Miss Mabel." Edward turned to her. "Could you help me stabilise..."

"Martha. Her name is Martha." Mabel said.

Edward nodded. "Can you help me stabilise Martha. She's the weaker of the two."

Together, they walked alongside the stretchers. Edward's presence brought a strange calm to their grim procession. He spoke softly to the unconscious girls, checking their breathing at regular intervals. When Martha's hand slipped from the makeshift bed, he caught it with such tenderness that Mabel's heart clenched.

The sound of boots and official voices filled the street before they reached the hospital. Men in dark coats approached, carrying documents and stern expressions.

"This area is under quarantine," one announced. "No one leaves until properly examined."

Mabel's stomach dropped. The basement room had been her only shelter, meagre as it was. Without it, she had nothing.

She watched helplessly as Edward argued with the officials, trying to secure passage for Lucy and Martha. The other workers huddled together, fear plain on their faces. Mabel's thoughts flew to Emma and Henry, safe in their beds at the orphanage. How could she help them now? How could she keep her promise?

The officials began separating them into groups, checking for symptoms. Edward's reassuring presence drifted away as he was led toward a different examination area. Mabel stood alone, watching her world crumble once again.

A NEW CHANCE

*M*abel stood on the street corner, clutching her mother's tablecloth to her chest as the quarantine officials waved her away. The evening air bit through her thin dress, and the cobblestones felt unsteady beneath her feet. No symptoms, they'd said. She was free to go — but where?

A familiar leather-bound book pressed against her side, hidden in the folds of her skirts. Edward's medical journal. She'd kept it safe through the chaos, and now it might give her one last chance to —

"Miss Mabel?"

Edward's voice cut through her thoughts. He approached from the quarantine line.

"Mr Montague." She pulled the journal from her dress. "I kept this safe for you."

His eyes widened as he took the book. "You protected this through everything?" He took the journal from her gently. "I can't thank you enough. These notes are invaluable to my studies."

"It was the least I could do, after your help with Lucy and Martha."

"Where will you go now? Surely not back to that basement?"

Mabel's shoulders dropped. "I don't know. I have nowhere else I can go, but I need to for—" She stopped herself from mentioning Emma and Henry.

Edward's expression shifted. "The Montague townhouse needs a new housemaid. I could speak to Miss Bachman, our housekeeper." He straightened his coat. "I'm sure with a good word from me, she'll be able to find you a place."

Mabel's heart jumped. The Montague townhouse — she'd passed it once, its windows gleaming like mirrors in the sunlight. A position there would mean regular wages, a proper bed, perhaps enough to help Emma and Henry.

"Would you really do that?" Her voice barely rose above a whisper.

"Consider it done. You saved my notes — let me help save your future."

THE MONTAGUE FAMILY

*T*he coach wheels clattered against cobblestones as Edward guided Mabel toward the Montague townhouse. Her mother's tablecloth pressed against her side, hidden beneath her worn dress. The house loomed before them, its cream-colored stone facade stretching upward like a mountain of wealth. Ornate moldings framed each window, their delicate patterns reminding Mabel of the lace she'd spent countless hours creating.

Edward helped her down from the coach. Mabel's boots touched the spotless front steps, and she fought the urge to check them for mud. Above the entrance, carved lions held shields bearing the Montague family crest.

A footman in a pressed uniform opened the heavy oak door. His gaze swept over Mabel's simple dress and patched shawl.

"Name?" The footman's voice carried the crisp authority of someone used to sorting the worthy from the unworthy.

Lady Rowena's words echoed in Mabel's mind — how she'd sneered at the Fairchild name when purchasing the collar. "Downs," Mabel whispered. "Mabel Downs."

Edward led her through the entrance hall, their footsteps

echoing against marble floors polished to a mirror shine. Crystal chandeliers caught the afternoon light, scattering rainbow patterns across silk wallpaper. Oil paintings of stern-faced ancestors watched their progress, each frame more elaborate than the last.

Fresh flowers filled porcelain vases taller than Henry, their perfume mixing with beeswax and leather. A grand staircase curved upward, its mahogany banister gleaming like liquid copper. Through open doorways, Mabel glimpsed velvet chairs, gilt mirrors, and delicate tables that would have fed her family for a year.

Edward led Mabel into a study lined with leather-bound books and maps. Lord Nathaniel Montague sat behind a massive oak desk, his quill scratching against parchment. Papers scattered across the surface like autumn leaves. He didn't look up.

"Father, this is Mabel. The one I've recommended to Miss Bachman for the housemaid position."

Lord Montague's quill paused. His dark eyes flicked up, then back to his work. "Very well."

"She has experience in domestic service and comes highly regarded for her attention to detail."

"I trust your judgment." Lord Montague sounded distracted. He shuffled through a stack of documents. "Miss Bachman will see to her duties. The estate requires particular attention with your mother gone these past years."

The study door opened. A young man who look strikingly like Edward strode in, his presence filling the room like smoke. His tailored suit emphasised his commanding height. Their eyes met briefly — he carried the sharp focus of a man who knew exactly what he wanted from the world.

"Hello, William." Edward said.

"Hello, brother." William turned to his father. "Father, the parliamentary papers require your signature." William's gaze settled on Mabel. "Good morning."

Mabel dropped into a small curtsy. "Good morning, sir."

William acknowledged her with a slight nod before turning back to his father. Her pulse quickened, but thoughts of Emma and Henry steadied her. This position meant survival, nothing more.

"Send this girl... Mabel, to Miss Bachman," Lord Montague waved his hand, already absorbed in the papers William had brought. "She'll show the girl her duties."

THE LACEMAKER'S DREAM

*M*iss Bachman stood in the servant's hall, her spine rigid as a fireplace poker. Her hazel eyes traced every detail of Mabel's appearance, from her threadbare dress to her worn boots.

"So." Miss Bachman's mouth tightened. "You're the one Master Edward found at that lace shop." She circled Mabel like a hawk studying its prey. "We maintain certain standards here at the Montague household. Standards that must be upheld regardless of how one comes to be employed."

Mabel's fingers brushed against the hidden tablecloth beneath her dress. "Yes, ma'am."

"Your hands." Miss Bachman seized Mabel's wrist, turning her palm upward. "Too soft for proper cleaning. We'll soon fix that." She released Mabel's hand. "Follow me."

The kitchen gleamed with copper pots and stone floors worn smooth by generations of servants' feet. Miss Bachman thrust a bucket and brush into Mabel's arms.

"Start with the entrance hall. On your knees, mind — properly scrubbed, not just wiped. Then the morning room needs dusting, every surface, including behind the ornaments. After that, the dinner dishes need washing. You also need to change into respectable clothes. You'll find two uniforms on your bed in the attic. Always keep them neat and clean."

Mabel's knees ached against the cold marble as she scrubbed. The brush bristles scraped her palms raw, nothing like the delicate movements of creating lace. Soap water seeped through her apron where she knelt, but she didn't dare pause. Miss Bachman's footsteps echoed nearby, checking corners and edges with sharp attention.

In the morning room, Mabel's arms trembled as she stretched to reach high shelves lined with delicate porcelain. Each piece cost more than she'd earned in months at Finch's shop. The feather duster disturbed motes that danced in sunbeams streaming through tall windows, making her think of Emma's drawings of fairy lights.

The kitchen's heat pressed against her face as she tackled mountains of dishes, her fingers pruning in the scalding water. These tasks felt worlds away from the precise, artistic work she'd done before, but she thought of her siblings and pressed on.

MABEL'S back screamed as she hauled water up the service stairs. Her third trip this morning, and still the copper bath wasn't full. The buckets pulled at her shoulders, water sloshing against her skirts. She paused on the landing, pressing her forehead against the cool wallpaper, careful not to let Miss Bachman catch her moment of weakness.

In the blue drawing room, she kept her eyes lowered as she swept beneath the velvet chairs. Lord Montague's voice carried from his study across the hall, discussing railway investments with William. The carpet beneath her broom probably cost more than a year's wages at Finch's shop.

"The northern line expansion could secure our position in Parliament," William said. "Though Lady Rowena suggests—"

Mabel's hands tightened on the broom handle. She thought of her father's small collection of books, how he'd dreamed of Emma attending a proper ladies' school someday. Now Emma sketched with broken pencil stubs at the orphanage while Mabel cleaned rooms larger than their entire cottage.

The afternoon sun streamed through tall windows as she polished silver in the dining room. Crystal glasses caught the light, scattering rainbow patterns across the mahogany table. Her mother's lace tablecloth would have looked beautiful here. Instead, it remained hidden in her narrow attic room, wrapped in brown paper, while she scrubbed and cleaned in silence.

Her arms ached, but she didn't dare slow down. Miss Bachman's footsteps could appear at any moment, checking for missed spots or smudged surfaces. The clock's steady ticking marked endless hours of labor, punctuated only by the distant sounds of the family's comfortable life — piano music from the morning room, tea cups clinking in the parlour, discussions of balls and garden parties floating down the halls.

In one of the short rest times she was allowed, Mabel sank onto her narrow bed. She retrieved her small notebook, its pages worn from constant handling. Between household accounts and cleaning schedules, delicate sketches filled the margins — forget-me-nots twining with roses, sparrows taking flight through loops of Brussels lace. Her pencil moved across the paper, adding depth to a half-finished design of ivy leaves.

The clock in the servants' hall struck ten. Mabel's shoulders ached from scrubbing floors and carrying coal, but her hands remained steady as she worked. Each stroke of the pencil defied her exhaustion, each pattern a reminder of who she was beyond these walls. Miss Bachman might see only a housemaid, but in these quiet moments, Mabel reclaimed her identity as an artist.

Tomorrow would bring more tasks, more scrutiny from

Miss Bachman's watchful eye. Yet Mabel welcomed the challenge. Every polished banister and spotless window proved her capability, showed she could thrive even here.

She sketched faster now, adding delicate ferns unfurling between the ivy. In her mind's eye, she saw Emma bent over her own drawings, Henry crafting wooden frames for their work. The three of them together again, creating beauty from the lessons their parents had taught them. The vision sustained her, making the endless hours of labor worthwhile.

The candle guttered, casting shadows across her notebook. Mabel closed it gently, tucking away her dreams until tomorrow. She might spend her days as a servant, but her heart remained that of a lacemaker, carrying forward her mother's legacy, stitch by precious stitch.

Mabel then retrieved her writing paper from beneath her thin mattress. The single candle cast just enough light to write by, though her eyes strained after the long day of cleaning.

She dipped her pen carefully into the inkwell, mindful not to spill a drop on her bedsheet.

"My dearest Emma and Henry," she wrote, her hand steady despite her fatigue. "I hope this letter finds you well. The work here is hard but honest. Each morning I think of you both as I polish the silver — how Henry would love the intricate patterns on the serving dishes, and how Emma would capture them perfectly in her drawings."

Mabel paused, touching the corner of her eye where moisture threatened to fall. "I've made a friend here, though you wouldn't believe it from our first meeting. James, the footman, looked right through me that first day. But yesterday he shared his bread with me when I missed supper due to extra cleaning, and today he told me stories about his own sister at school while we polished boots together."

She wrote of the grand rooms she cleaned, describing them in detail so Emma could imagine drawing them. For Henry, she included funny little stories about the kitchen cat who stole fish when the cook wasn't looking.

A soft knock at her door made her start. James stood there, his formal demeanour softened by the late hour.

"I'm heading to post a letter for his lordship first thing tomorrow," he whispered. "I could take yours too, if you'd like."

Mabel quickly signed her name and sealed the envelope. "Thank you, James. It means more than I can say."

He took the letter with a gentle smile. "We all have someone we miss, don't we? Get some rest, Mabel. Tomorrow's another long day."

THE HOUGHTON LADIES

*M*abel's arms burned from scrubbing the entrance hall's marble floor when the distinct sound of carriage wheels on cobblestones caught her attention. The noise grew louder, accompanied by the clip-clop of horses' hooves drawing near the Montague townhouse.

James pushed open the grand front doors, and stepped out. A magnificent black carriage pulled up, its polished surface gleaming in the light. The footman leapt forward to assist the passengers, and Lady Rowena Houghton emerged with practiced grace. Her gown, a rich burgundy silk, featured delicate Brussels lace at the collar and cuffs — the same pattern Mabel had created in Finch's basement workroom.

A younger woman followed, who could only be Cecilia Houghton. Her fingers wrapped around her mother's arm like pale spider legs. The girl's face twisted into a frown that marred her otherwise pretty features. Her golden curls bounced with each reluctant step.

"Do straighten up, darling," Lady Rowena murmured, her voice carrying across the quiet street. She offered a brilliant smile to the waiting servants, her eyes sweeping past Mabel without recognition.

Cecilia's lower lip jutted out. "I told you I wanted to arrive after tea."

The household staff moved with practiced efficiency around Mabel. Cook smoothed her apron, James adjusted his livery, and Beth the parlour maid ducked her head to hide a knowing smirk. They traded glances loaded with meaning, and whispers floated through the air like autumn leaves.

"Third visit this month," Beth breathed to James.

"Her ladyship's quite determined, isn't she?" James replied under his breath.

MABEL RAN the feather duster along the mahogany shelves in Lord Montague's study, her movements slowing as Ruth and Joan's voices drifted through the partially open door.

"It's all arranged, from what I hear," Ruth whispered as she worked. "Lady Rowena's been meeting with his lordship in private."

Joan clicked her tongue. "About young Master Edward and Miss Cecilia?"

"Lady Rowena's got it all planned out. His lordship thinks it's a fine match – combining the families would strengthen both estates."

"But what about Master Edward's medical work? He's hardly at home these days, always at that clinic of his."

"That's just it — they say once he's married, he'll have to take on proper responsibilities. Can't have a gentleman's son playing doctor forever."

The duster trembled in Mabel's hand. She'd seen Edward's passion for healing during the cholera outbreak, witnessed his gentle care for the sick workers. The thought of him being forced to abandon his calling made her chest tighten.

From her position near the study window, Mabel caught glimpses of the drawing room across the hall. Cecilia had draped herself dramatically across a chaise lounge, her golden curls arranged just so against the velvet cushions.

"It's dreadfully dull here," Cecilia announced to no one in particular, though her eyes darted to the doorway the moment Edward's footsteps echoed in the hall.

He entered carrying medical texts, and Cecilia's posture shifted subtly. Her sulk transformed into a coy smile as she touched her throat where the lace — Mabel's lace — adorned her collar.

"Edward, dear, you must tell me about your latest studies," Cecilia cooed, patting the seat beside her. "Though I warn you, all this talk of illness makes me terribly faint."

Lady Rowena watched from her armchair, satisfaction glinting in her eyes as Cecilia commanded Edward's attention with practiced ease. The whole scene played out like an elaborate dance, with Cecilia as the star performer and her mother the proud choreographer.

Mabel kept her eyes lowered as she worked, but her attention fixed on Edward's response to Cecilia's invitation. He barely glanced at the offered seat, instead spreading his medical texts across the side table.

"Actually, I've discovered fascinating research about preventing fever spread in cramped conditions. The implications for worker housing could save countless lives." His eyes lit up as he flipped through pages of careful notes.

Cecilia's practiced smile wavered. "But surely such matters are better left to... others." She adjusted her lace collar, fingers trailing along the pattern Mabel had crafted in those dark basement hours.

Edward didn't notice the gesture, already deep in explaining his findings. "Look here — proper ventilation systems could reduce mortality rates by half. I've drawn up plans to implement these in the clinic."

Lady Rowena's lips pressed into a thin line as Edward continued, his enthusiasm for medicine overwhelming Cecilia's attempts to redirect the conversation to more suitable topics for a gentleman's son.

Mabel's chest warmed watching him gesture animatedly about sanitation improvements. Where others saw improper fixation on common people's concerns, she recognised the pure heart driving his passion. No calculated social graces or false pretences — just genuine desire to ease suffering.

Cecilia shot her mother a helpless look as Edward pulled out detailed sketches of hospital layouts. Lady Rowena's carefully arranged scene crumbled before Edward's oblivious sincerity. He remained utterly absorbed in sharing his vision for better medical care, blind to the matrimonial web being woven around him.

A small smile tugged at Mabel's lips as she moved to dust another shelf. His earnest nature shielded him from seeing the manipulations at play — the same genuine spirit that had driven him to break down a locked door to help suffering workers.

DELICATE DANCE

*O*ver the weeks, Mabel watched the delicate dance unfold between Edward and the Houghtons. Lady Rowena's visits grew more frequent, each one orchestrated like moves in an elaborate game of chess. The staff's whispers painted a clear picture — Edward's medical ambitions clashed with the expectations being woven around him.

In quiet moments between her duties, Mabel caught glimpses of Edward's struggles. His shoulders tensed when talk turned to estate matters. His eyes dulled during discussions of proper society functions. Yet his face lit up whenever he spoke of his clinic work or shared medical journals with the kitchen boy who expressed interest in healing.

Mabel found herself lingering longer in rooms where Edward studied, straightening items that needed no straightening. She recognised the weight settling on his shoulders. The same burden she'd carried trying to protect Emma and Henry. Edward needed someone to guard his dreams as fiercely as she guarded her siblings.

That afternoon, while arranging flowers in the drawing room, Lady Rowena's voice drifted through the doorway. "My dear Edward, surely you see what a suitable match you and Cecilia would make. Your father agrees — combining our families would secure both estates' futures."

Mabel's fingers trembled around the stem of a rose.

"Your medical interests are admirable, of course," Lady Rowena continued, "but a gentleman of your standing has greater responsibilities. Cecilia understands the importance of maintaining proper society connections."

Mabel's heart pounded. She'd witnessed too many dreams crushed under the weight of obligation — her father's love of teaching destroyed by false accusations, her mother's artistic spirit dimmed by poverty. Now Edward's passion for healing teetered on the edge of being sacrificed to family duty and social expectations.

In the servants' hall, Mabel poured tea while Beth and Joan huddled close, their voices low but charged with knowing.

"Third time this week Lady Rowena's swooped in like a hawk," Beth muttered, adding sugar to her cup. "Poor Mr. Edward barely gets a moment's peace with his medical books before she appears."

Joan nodded, her weathered hands smoothing her apron. "She's got Lord Montague wrapped around her finger, she does. All those private meetings in his study, discussing 'estate matters.' More like plotting young Master Edward's future without his say."

Mabel's fingers tightened around the teapot handle. The familiar weight of powerlessness settled in her chest. It was the same feeling she'd carried watching Mr Ardon destroy her father's reputation.

"Mark my words," Ruth chimed in from her corner, darning a sock. "She's got plans for that daughter of hers. Saw her instructing Miss Cecilia on how to catch Master Edward's eye. 'Stand just so, dear. Laugh at his medical stories, even if you don't understand them.'"

The maids shared knowing looks. They'd all witnessed similar scenes play out in other households — wealthy families arranging marriages like business transactions.

"At least we can warn each other when she's coming," Beth offered, patting Mabel's hand. "Give Master Edward time to escape to his study if he needs."

Mabel found herself nodding, grateful for their small acts of resistance. These women understood what it meant to navigate between worlds, to protect what little control they had over their own lives.

"Remember when she demanded we re-polish the silver three times because it wasn't 'gleaming properly' for Miss Cecilia's visit?" Joan rolled her eyes. "As if that would make Master Edward notice her more."

Their shared laughter carried an edge of defiance. In these quiet moments between tasks, they formed their own kind of family — one built on understanding and mutual support.

DEPARTURE

*M*abel folded bedsheets, her fingers tracing the delicate embroidery while chaos erupted around her. Footmen hauled leather trunks down marble stairs. Maids scurried between rooms with armfuls of silk gowns and pressed linens. The air crackled with anticipation of the house's departure to Derbyshire. Not only was the Montague family going, but all their staff as well — including Mabel.

In the midst of the commotion, Mabel's thoughts drifted to Emma's latest letter. Her sister's careful drawings of orphanage flowers decorated the margins — proof of her artistic spirit surviving despite their separation. Henry had added a short note about learning to whittle wood from another boy. Such small victories, yet they meant everything.

The sound of Miss Bachman barking orders yanked Mabel back to her tasks. She moved through the drawing room, adjusting cushions and straightening picture frames while watching the parade of luggage through the doorway. Each trunk represented another mile between her and the orphanage gates where she'd promised to return.

Her weekly letters to Emma and Henry were an anchor —

the one constant in a life turned upside down. Now even that small comfort would slip away. The thought of their faces growing distant, of missing Henry's growth spurts or Emma's artistic progress, made her hands shake as she dusted the mantelpiece.

A maid rushed past with Lord Montague's riding boots. Another followed carrying William's parliamentary papers. The house buzzed like a disturbed beehive, everyone focused on the grand migration to come. No one noticed the housemaid in the corner, fighting back tears as she polished already gleaming silver, her world shrinking with each passing minute.

Through the window, Mabel watched footmen securing trunks to carriages. The familiar weight of powerlessness settled in her chest. Once again, circumstances beyond her control threatened to tear apart what remained of her family.

The house emptied as servants rushed to complete their tasks. Mabel sank onto the drawing room sofa, her fingers twisting her apron. The separation from Emma and Henry crushed against her chest.

"What if their letters get lost?" Her whisper barely disturbed the air. "What if they think I've abandoned them?" She bit her lip, fighting the tears that threatened to spill. The memory of Emma's hands clutching her skirts, of Henry's brave attempt at a smile as she'd left them at the orphanage, tore at her heart.

A floorboard creaked. Edward stood in the doorway, medical journal tucked under his arm. His brow furrowed as he caught sight of her distress. He lingered, watching as she hastily wiped her eyes with her sleeve.

"Miss Downs?" His voice carried gentle concern. He stepped into the room, closing the distance between them with measured steps.

Mabel hastily smoothed her apron, mortified to be caught in such a state by the young master. Her heart fluttered as Edward approached, his medical journal tucked beneath his arm.

"What troubles you?" He sounded genuinely concerned rather than merely polite.

Mabel's fingers twisted in her apron. "My siblings, sir. Emma and Henry — they're at Hampstead Orphanage. I've been writing to them each week, but now..." She swallowed hard. "With the family moving to Derbyshire, I fear the letters won't reach them. They're so young, you see..." Her voice caught.

"The position here has been such a blessing," Mabel added quickly, not wanting to seem ungrateful. "Miss Bachman's strict but fair, and the wages help ensure they're cared for. It's just..." She glanced at the window where another trunk was being secured to a carriage. "They've already lost so much. Our mother, our father imprisoned..." She pressed her lips together, realising she'd revealed too much in her distress.

"I promised to keep them safe, to return for them once I had proper work. If they think I've abandoned them..." Mabel's voice faded as she fought back fresh tears.

Edward stepped closer, his shadow falling across the polished floor. "Your dedication to them is admirable, Miss Downs."

Mabel flinched at the false name, guilt mingling with her worry. But the kindness in his voice made her look up, meeting his concerned gaze.

"The wages here — they've meant regular meals for them, proper clothes. Mrs Winters at the orphanage says Henry's even learning carpentry now. I'm so grateful for the position, truly. I just..." She smoothed her apron again, steadying herself. "I cannot bear the thought of losing contact with them."

"I give you my word — I'll make sure your letters reach them." Edward's eyes held steady with hers. "I have contacts in London who can ensure they're delivered safely. Every single one."

"You would do that?"

"Of course." He smiled, the warmth reaching his eyes. "Family should never lose touch, no matter the distance."

Hope flickered in Mabel, small but bright. She looked up at Edward, seeing not just the wealthy son of Lord Montague, but someone who truly understood the depth of her fear. His promise wrapped around her like a warm shawl, offering protection against the uncertainty ahead.

Mabel's heart fluttered as she looked up at Edward, his promise wrapping around her like a protective shield. For the first time since leaving Emma and Henry, someone truly understood. Not just her circumstances, but her deepest fears about losing them. The genuine concern in his eyes made her feel seen — not as a housemaid, but as a sister fighting to keep her family together. She drew in a shaky breath, preparing to thank him for his kindness.

"Edward." Lady Rowena's voice cut through the moment like a blade. She glided into the drawing room, her burgundy skirts rustling against the carpet. "I hardly think it appropriate for you to concern yourself with servant matters, especially with the Season approaching." Her words carried the weight of social expectation, sharp and precise.

The warmth that had bloomed in Mabel's chest withered. She quickly arose from the sofa and stepped back, the familiar walls of class distinction rising between them once more. Lady Rowena's calculated tone left no room for argument — this was not Mabel's world, and she had dared to forget her place.

Edward's jaw tightened as he turned toward Lady Rowena. His medical journal shifted in his grip, knuckles whitening slightly. The struggle played across his features — duty warring with compassion as Lady Rowena's presence filled the room with unspoken demands.

Mabel caught the flash of something cold in Lady Rowena's eyes. The lady's perfectly composed expression slipped for just a moment, revealing a calculating anger that chilled Mabel to her core. She watched as Lady Rowena's gaze darted between them, assessing the threat to her carefully laid plans.

The tenderness Edward had shown while promising to help with the letters seemed to wound Lady Rowena deeply. Her fingers tightened around her fan, the only outward sign of her inner turmoil as she witnessed the genuine connection forming between Edward and the housemaid — a connection that threatened to derail her ambitions for the Montague family's future.

Mabel straightened her spine, jaw set with quiet determination. She'd survived Finch's basement, the workhouse, and countless rejections. This too would not break her. Edward's promise to help with the letters kindled a small flame of hope. She would find ways to reach Emma and Henry.

Edward rose from the sofa, but hesitated as he passed by Lady Rowena. His eyes met Mabel's briefly, carrying an apology he couldn't voice. The muscle in his jaw twitched as Lady Rowena laid a proprietary hand on his arm, steering him toward the door with practiced grace.

Watching him leave, Mabel pressed her hand against her heart where his promise still echoed. The ache of longing mingled with determination. She might be just a housemaid in Lady Rowena's eyes, but she was also Mary Fairchild's daughter, Thomas Fairchild's eldest, Emma and Henry's protector. No amount of social pressure could erase those truths from her soul.

The front steps of the Montague townhouse gleamed in the light as footmen secured the last of the trunks. Mabel stood back from the bustle, her hands clasped tightly before her apron. The familiar weight of her mother's tablecloth, hidden beneath her dress, pressed against her skin — a constant reminder of who she was and where she came from.

Lord Montague emerged first, his commanding presence drawing immediate attention. William followed, already discussing parliamentary matters with his father. Lady Rowena hovered near the doorway, ensuring Cecilia was positioned perfectly as Edward descended the steps, medical journal still tucked under his arm. The Houghton estate just so happened to be close-by to the Montague's, so Lady Rowena and Cecilia would be travelling home alongside them all. Lady Rowena had made it out to seem like a happy coincidence, but almost everyone was aware that it was a perfectly planned ploy.

Through the grand entrance hall, the echoes of "Safe journey" and "Godspeed" bounced off marble floors. Miss Bachman directed the remaining servants with sharp efficiency, but Mabel barely heard the instructions. Her thoughts drifted to Emma's latest drawings and Henry's proud notes about his woodworking progress.

The morning sun caught the brass fixtures of the carriage, nearly blinding in their brilliance. Mabel blinked, remembering the much dimmer light of Finch's basement, the darkness of the workhouse. She'd survived those trials. This new challenge — distance from her siblings — would not defeat her either.

Edward paused at the carriage door, glancing back. Their eyes met briefly across the social divide that Lady Rowena had so firmly reinforced. But in that moment, Mabel felt steel enter her spine. She might be just a housemaid in their world, but she was also taught to create beauty from mere threads. That same strength would help her weave together the scattered pieces of her family, no matter the distance.

As the carriages pulled away, Mabel touched the hidden tablecloth, drawing comfort from its familiar patterns. Love, she knew, could cross any distance. It had sustained her through the workhouse, through leaving Emma and Henry at the orphanage. It would sustain her still, as she found new ways to keep her family connected despite the miles between them.

THE MONTAGUE ESTATE

*T*he servants' carriage rattled up the winding drive of
the Montague estate, each turn revealing new wonders
that stole Mabel's breath. Stone pillars rose like sentinels against
the autumn sky, their weathered faces telling tales of generations
past. Ornate windows caught the morning light, transforming the
grand house into a jewel set among emerald lawns.

Mabel's fingers found the hidden folds of her mother's tablecloth beneath her dress as the carriage approached the servants'
entrance. The mansion's elegant architecture dwarfed even her
most ambitious dreams — carved cornices traced delicate
patterns across the façade, while climbing roses wove their way
up trellises like nature's own lacework.

Through gaps in the manicured hedges, she glimpsed foun-
tains spraying silver threads into the air. Gardens stretched
toward distant woods, their paths lined with late-blooming
flowers that reminded her of the patterns she'd once sketched
beside Emma.

The carriage crested a rise, and Mabel's heart caught at the
view spread before her. Rolling hills swept down toward

Ashbourne village, its church spire piercing the morning mist like a needle through silk. The Houghton estate sat proud on a distant rise, its grounds bleeding into dense woodland.

Pine-scented air filled her lungs, so different from London's sooty breath. The familiar ache of loss mingled with the crisp morning breeze.

Beyond the village, factory chimneys rose from Derby's outskirts, their smoke barely visible against the pale sky. Somewhere in that direction lay Emma and Henry, separated from her by more than just miles. Mabel pressed her hand against the window glass, tracing the path her letters would need to travel to reach them.

Miss Bachman gathered the servants in the grand entrance hall, her stern gaze sweeping across the assembled staff. Sunlight streamed through tall windows, casting long shadows across the marble floor.

"New assignments for the season." Miss Bachman's voice echoed. "Beth, you'll assist Cook. James and Laurence, footman duties remain unchanged." She paused at Mabel. "Mabel, you're to attend Lady Clara Montague, newly arrived from Brighton. She is the Lord's niece, and she requires a lady's maid with... particular skills."

Mabel's heart quickened. A lady's maid — the position would demand more than the basic household duties she'd performed in London.

Clara Montague swept into the entrance hall like a fresh breeze, her green eyes bright with warmth. "Oh, you must be my new maid!" She clasped Mabel's hands in greeting, ignoring Miss Bachman's raised eyebrow at such familiarity. "I've heard wonderful things about your needlework."

The genuine warmth in Clara's voice eased some of the tension in Mabel's shoulders.

"Come, I'll show you my wardrobe." Clara led the way

upstairs, chattering about Brighton's sea air and her excitement to spend time with her cousins.

In Clara's chambers, Mabel unpacked trunks filled with silks and muslins in shades of cream, rose, and spring green. Her fingers traced delicate embroidery as she hung each dress with care. The room itself spoke of refined taste — pale blue wallpaper, elegant furniture, and windows that caught the morning light.

"These need pressing before tonight's dinner," Clara indicated a selection of evening gowns. "But first, could you help me choose accessories for this afternoon? Edward mentioned a walk through the gardens, and I want to look my best."

Mabel selected a pale pink ribbon that complemented Clara's complexion, her movements precise as she arranged Clara's hair. The familiar work of smoothing fabric and adjusting trims helped steady her nerves, even as she felt the weight of her new responsibilities.

Through Clara's window, Mabel watched Edward cross the garden path below. He paused to examine a cluster of late roses, and her heart quickened at the gentle way he touched the petals — so different from his brother William's stern stride or his father's commanding presence.

"He's quite remarkable, isn't he?" Clara's voice carried no judgment, only warmth. "Always rushing off to tend someone in the village when Uncle wants him reviewing estate papers."

Mabel smoothed the wrinkles from Clara's dress, keeping her eyes lowered. "Your cousin seems very dedicated to his work, my lady."

"Oh please, just Clara when we're alone." Clara turned from the window. "And you must tell me about your lacemaking. Edward mentioned you worked at Finch's Lace Shop? I never liked that man, but you must have been quite good with lace-making to get a position there!"

The kindness in Clara's tone loosened something within

Mabel. As she arranged Clara's hair with practiced movements, she shared small details about different lace patterns, careful to avoid mentions of Finch's shop or her family's past.

Clara's enthusiasm for Mabel's craft reminded her of Emma's wide-eyed wonder when learning new stitches. The thought of her sister brought both comfort and pain – but Edward's promise about the letters eased her worry. Just that morning, she'd seen him hand a sealed envelope to his London messenger, giving specific instructions about its delivery to Hampstead.

"There," Mabel said, securing the final pin in Clara's hair. "The ribbon complements your complexion perfectly."

Clara beamed at her reflection. "You have a true gift, Mabel. I can see why Edward spoke so highly of your skills."

The mention of Edward's name sent warmth to Mabel's cheeks, but she focused on straightening Clara's lace cuffs. In this bright room, with Clara's genuine appreciation and Edward's silent support, Mabel felt the first stirrings of hope since leaving London. Here, perhaps, she could build something worthy of Emma and Henry's future.

LIFE IN DERBYSHIRE

*M*abel smoothed the wrinkles from Clara's evening gown, her fingers trembling as Miss Bachman's footsteps clicked across the parquet floor behind her. The housekeeper's reflection appeared in the mirror, hawk-like eyes tracking each movement of Mabel's hands.

"The sleeve pleats need more attention." Miss Bachman's voice cut through the air. "And mind you don't snag the silk with those rough fingers."

Heat crept up Mabel's neck as she adjusted the delicate fabric. The previous day's misstep with the tea service still burned in her memory — Miss Bachman's sharp intake of breath when Mabel had nearly stumbled on the library threshold.

"That will do for now." Miss Bachman's lips pressed into a thin line. "The silver needs polishing before dinner."

Clara waited until Miss Bachman's footsteps faded before turning to Mabel. "Don't let her frighten you. She was just as stern with my last lady's maid." She touched Mabel's arm gently. "Here, let me show you a trick for managing those pleats — something I learned from watching the dressmakers in

Brighton."

Mabel's shoulders relaxed as Clara demonstrated the technique, her warm voice explaining each step. These quiet moments with Clara felt like islands of peace in the sea of watchful eyes and whispered critiques that filled the halls.

"You're doing wonderfully," Clara said, admiring her now-perfect sleeve. "And I've noticed how quickly you've learned the household schedules. That's no small feat in a house this size."

The praise settled something in Mabel's chest, even as Miss Bachman's shadow darkened another doorway. Clara's kindness reminded her of those precious hours spent teaching Emma new stitches – moments when judgment fell away and only the work remained.

"Thank you, my lady," Mabel whispered, though her heart spoke louder: *Thank you for seeing me.*

Clara's enthusiasm for life at the estate transformed Mabel's daily routines into moments of unexpected joy. When Clara invited Mabel to help arrange flowers for afternoon tea, Mabel found herself sharing suggestions about which blooms might complement the china patterns.

"These white roses would look lovely against the blue porcelain," Mabel said, carefully trimming stems.

"You have such an eye for detail." Clara beamed, gathering more flowers from the basket.

The familiar work of creating beauty from simple elements awakened something in Mabel that had lain dormant since her days in the cottage with her mother. She began suggesting small touches — lavender sprigs in guest rooms, fresh wildflowers on breakfast trays – that earned approving nods from Clara and even occasional praise from Miss Bachman.

During these preparations, Edward's presence in the house stirred different emotions in Mabel. He'd pause in doorways while she worked, offering quiet good mornings that felt more like conversations than mere greetings. Once, when she struggled with a heavy vase, he stepped forward to steady it.

"Careful there," he said softly, his hands brushing hers as he helped set it down. "These old vases are treacherous things."

His touch lingered a moment longer than necessary, and Mabel felt warmth spread through her chest. In these brief encounters, she glimpsed the same person who'd broken down that basement door — someone who saw past stations and circumstances to the humanity beneath.

These moments left Mabel's heart torn between hope and duty. Each letter she wrote to Emma and Henry renewed her sense of responsibility, yet Edward's kindness made her wonder if perhaps she could hold both — her promise to her siblings and these newfound feelings that brightened her days like sunlight through chapel windows.

In her attic room, Mabel traced her fingers over Emma's latest drawing — a cluster of daisies pressed between the pages of her letter. The candlelight caught the dried petals, casting delicate shadows across the paper. Her sister's artistic touch had grown stronger, even in the confines of the orphanage.

Henry's words filled the opposite page, his slightly lopsided script detailing his latest woodworking project — a small box he'd carved under Mrs Winters' supervision. Pride swelled in Mabel at his determination to continue their father's craft.

Every Sunday evening, after her duties, Mabel would sit at her small desk and pour her heart onto paper. She told them about Clara's kindness, the gardens that reminded her of their mother's beloved flowers, and the small victories she achieved each day. She kept her tone bright, focusing on hopes rather than hardships.

The letters became her sanctuary, a place where she could be both sister and guardian, sharing pieces of her new world while holding fast to their old one. She described the estate's grandeur in ways that would make Emma gasp and Henry laugh – the marble fireplaces that could fit their old cottage's hearth three times over, the library shelves that stretched toward heaven.

Edward's quiet dedication to their correspondence touched something deep in Mabel's heart. Each week, without fail, he would ensure her letters reached London. Sometimes he'd appear at her door with a reply, his eyes warm with understanding as he handed over the precious envelopes.

"Your sister's artistic talent shines through," he'd observed once, noticing Emma's pressed flower falling from a letter. "She has your eye for beauty."

These moments of connection, brief though they were, strengthened Mabel's resolve. Each small success in the household, each word of praise from Clara or grudging approval from Miss Bachman, felt like stepping stones toward her ultimate goal – a future where she could provide Emma and Henry with the stability and opportunities they deserved.

PREPARATION FOR THE SEASON

*M*abel folded the last of Clara's evening gowns, smoothing each crease with practiced care. The estate hummed with activity — footmen rushing around, maids beating dust from carpets, and Cook barking orders about menu preparations. Even the air felt charged, weighted with expectations of the approaching social season.

Through the dressing room window, she glimpsed carriages arriving with boxes from London's finest shops. Each delivery brought new gowns, accessories, and fineries that would transform the already grand house into a stage for society's elaborate dance.

Her fingers traced the delicate beadwork on Clara's newest ball gown. The craftsmanship reminded her of long hours spent creating lace, each bead like a tiny stitch building toward something greater. Now, instead of creating beauty, she preserved it — ensuring Clara's wardrobe remained immaculate and ready for whatever social occasion arose.

Miss Bachman's steps echoed in the corridor, checking on preparations. Mabel straightened Clara's hair ribbons by colour and shade, knowing the housekeeper's eye for detail would catch any imperfection. The morning light caught the silver brush set she'd polished earlier, throwing sparkles across the wall.

"The blue silk needs pressing again," Mabel muttered to herself, noting how the fabric had settled in its drawer. She'd learned that such attention to detail could mean the difference between praise and censure in this world of careful observations and subtle judgments.

In the midst of organising Clara's gloves by length and occasion, Mabel found herself planning ahead — which accessories would best suit which events, how to arrange the jewellery box for quickest access during rushed changes. These small efficiencies might go unnoticed by most, but they would help Clara navigate the demanding social calendar with grace.

The work steadied her, gave purpose to her days beyond mere survival. Each perfectly arranged drawer and gleaming surface felt like a small victory, a step toward proving her worth in this grand house where every action carried weight.

FRAGILE WORLDS

*T*he gravel crunched beneath the wheels of Lady Rowena's carriage as it swept up the drive for the third time that week. Mabel paused in her task of arranging flowers, watching through the window as the footmen rushed to assist. Lady Rowena emerged first, her burgundy silk dress catching the morning light. Cecilia followed, her golden curls arranged in the latest London fashion.

The household staff straightened as Lady Rowena's perfume wafted through the entrance hall. Her melodic laugh drifted up from below as Lord Nathaniel greeted them, his usual stern demeanour softening under her practiced charm. Mabel recognized the careful orchestration in Lady Rowena's movements — each gesture and tilt of her head calculated to draw attention.

"My dear Nathaniel," Lady Rowena's voice carried up the stairs, "you must tell me more about your plans for expanding the estate's holdings."

Cecilia didn't join her mother's conversation. Instead, she wandered the drawing room, adjusting her skirts to catch the light whenever Edward passed nearby. Her attempts at appearing absorbed in a book fooled no one — the volume remained open to the same page for over an hour.

"Miss Houghton certainly has a way about her," Beth whispered to Joan as they polished the silver. "Though if you ask me, there's something practiced in those pretty smiles."

Mabel observed Cecilia's performance from the corner where she mended Clara's gloves. The young woman's laugh tinkled like glass bells when Edward mentioned his medical studies, though her eyes glazed over at the actual content of his words. She touched his arm, let her handkerchief drop — small actions that seemed lifted from a guide to feminine wiles rather than genuine interest.

The other maids exchanged knowing looks as they went about their duties. Everyone understood the dance taking place — the careful positioning of Cecilia in Edward's path, Lady Rowena's strategic conversations with Lord Nathaniel about combining estates and securing futures. It played out like a carefully choreographed ballet, with only Edward seemingly unaware of his assigned role.

Mabel carried fresh linens past the library when she spotted Edward hunched over architectural drawings. Papers scattered across the mahogany table, his fingers ink-stained as he sketched layouts for the Ashbourne clinic. Dark circles shadowed his eyes, evidence of late nights spent planning rather than attending his father's business meetings.

"Miss Downs," he called out, noticing her. "Your eye for detail would be invaluable here."

She hesitated, but his earnest expression drew her in. He spread out the drawings, explaining his vision for examination rooms and a waiting area that would welcome even the poorest villagers.

"The space needs to feel dignified," Edward said, running a hand through his disheveled hair. "But practical too. What are your thoughts?"

Mabel traced the lines with her finger, remembering the workhouse infirmary's crushing atmosphere. "Perhaps separate entrances for different ailments? And windows here would bring natural light, making it less intimidating."

Edward's face lit up. He grabbed a fresh sheet, quickly incorporating her suggestions. "Brilliant! And what about the layout for storing medical supplies?"

The excitement in his voice matched the spark she felt suggesting improvements. Soon they were deep in discussion about efficient arrangements and welcoming touches that would put patients at ease. Edward valued her practical knowledge, gained from years of managing tight spaces in their cottage.

"Your creative mind sees solutions I miss entirely," he said, studying the revised plans. "This will help so many families."

The praise warmed her chest. She found herself sharing ideas about incorporating artwork to brighten the waiting area, describing how her mother's lace had brought beauty to their humble home. Edward listened intently, his genuine interest in her perspective making her forget their different stations.

"You understand exactly what I'm trying to achieve," he said softly. "A place of healing that honours human dignity."

Mabel nodded, watching his hands sketch another adjustment. His dedication to serving others resonated deeply with her own dreams of creating beauty that uplifted people's spirits.

Edward gathered the revised clinic drawings, careful not to smudge the precise lines.

As Mabel stepped into the corridor, Sarah's knowing smile made her cheeks warm.

"Quite the architect's assistant you've become," Sarah whispered, adjusting her apron with exaggerated care. The other maids nearby ducked their heads to hide their grins.

In the servant's hall, Beth and Joan's conversation halted as Mabel entered. Beth's eyebrows lifted as she folded linens, her gaze following Mabel across the room. "Our Miss Downs certainly has a gift for hospital design," she murmured, just loud enough to carry.

Mabel focused on arranging the tea service, but couldn't miss the meaningful glances exchanged between the housemaids. Their whispers followed her up the back stairs — snippets about "natural chemistry" and "the young master's new confidante" floating in her wake.

Even Miss Bachman's stern expression held a hint of concern as she watched Mabel deliver fresh flowers to the library where Edward worked. The housekeeper's lips pressed into a thin line when Edward asked Mabel's opinion on another drawing, their heads bent together over the desk.

Lady Rowena's reaction cut sharper than the servants' gentle teasing. Her smile remained fixed as she observed Edward and Mabel discussing ventilation designs, but her fingers gripped her fan until the delicate wood creaked. When Edward praised Mabel's suggestion about the waiting room layout, Lady Rowena's laugh held an edge like cracking ice.

"How... quaint," Lady Rowena said, each word precise as a pin prick, "to seek advice from the help." Her eyes swept over Mabel's plain unform. "Though I suppose one must find amusement where one can."

Mabel kept her face carefully blank as she gathered the tea things, feeling the weight of both the servants' speculation and Lady Rowena's calculated disdain. She tucked away the warmth of working with Edward, knowing it belonged to a world as fragile as tissue paper.

SUPPORT

*M*abel watched Edward rub his temples, his shoulders tense as he pored over the clinic plans. Lord Montague's voice drifted through the library door, discussing railway investments with William. Edward's jaw tightened at each mention of "family duty" and "proper connections."

Her fingers itched to smooth the worry from his brow. Instead, she adjusted the curtains, letting in more natural light over his workspace. His quiet "thank you" carried a deeper gratitude.

Lady Rowena swept into the room, Cecilia trailing behind like a pale shadow. "Edward, darling. The Fallingtons are hosting a garden party. Cecilia would love your company."

Edward barely glanced up from his sketches. "My apologies, but I have things that require my attention."

Mabel's heart fluttered as Lady Rowena's smile frosted over. The woman's fingers drummed against her fan while Cecilia wilted further.

"Surely you can spare an afternoon for society," Lady

Rowena pressed. "Your father agrees these connections are vital for your future."

Edward's pen paused mid-stroke. His shoulders stiffened, but he kept his voice level. "The clinic's future is vital to dozens of families who need proper medical care."

Mabel busied herself with dusting the shelves, each swipe of her cloth a silent show of support. She recognised the same fierce devotion to family in his dedication to the village that drove her own promise to Emma and Henry.

"The staff whispers, you know," Lady Rowena said softly. "About your... unusual priorities."

Edward finally looked up, his grey eyes tired but determined. "Let them whisper. I'd rather earn their respect through action than their approval through pretence."

His gaze caught Mabel's for a moment. In that brief connection, she saw the same understanding that had sparked between them over clinic designs and patient needs – a shared belief in practical care over social performance.

Lady Rowena left in a rustle of silk and displeasure. Edward returned to his work, but his pen moved with renewed purpose. Mabel noticed his breathing had steadied, as if their silent alliance had somehow lightened his burden.

MABEL CIRCLED the dining table with a crystal decanter, refilling wine glasses while keeping her movements fluid and silent. Candlelight caught the rubies at Lady Rowena's throat — their deep red matching the frustration that coloured her cheeks as Edward discussed village health concerns with Dr Harrison rather than responding to Cecilia's attempts at conversation.

"The mortality rates among mill workers is shocking," Edward said, his voice carrying passion rather than the expected dinner pleasantries. "With proper ventilation and basic medical care—"

"Perhaps we could discuss lighter topics," Lady Rowena interrupted, her charm wearing thin. "Cecilia has been studying new piano pieces, haven't you dear?"

Cecilia's fingers twisted in her lap. "Yes, mother. Though I find myself quite occupied with watercolours lately."

Edward nodded politely but turned back to Dr Harrison. Mabel noticed how Lady Rowena's knuckles whitened around her fork.

The familiar patterns of society played out before her — the careful manoeuvres, the strategic alliances, the subtle warfare beneath silk and silver. Mabel recognised them all while remaining invisible, just another shadow moving between the bright spots of conversation.

Her heart ached watching Edward defend his vision for the clinic. His dedication to helping others reminded her so much of her own drive to protect Emma and Henry. She pushed aside the warmth that spread through her chest when he spoke with such conviction. Her role was to support his dreams, not entertain impossible ones of her own.

Later, as she cleared dessert plates, she caught fragments of Edward's plans for the clinic layout. Her mind raced with possibilities — ways to arrange rooms for maximum light and air flow, how to create comfort through simple beauty. She'd seen how her mother's lace brought peace to weary hearts. Perhaps her art could do the same for Edward's patients.

The thought sustained her through the rest of service, even as Lady Rowena's sharp glances cut across the room. Mabel had found her own way to help — not through grand gestures or social connections, but through the quiet power of creating beauty in unexpected places.

GARDEN PARTY

*R*oses climbed the garden trellises in vibrant cascades of pink and white, their perfume mingling with the sweetness of fresh-cut grass. Mabel wove between the scattered tables, each draped in pristine linen and adorned with silver that caught the afternoon sun. Crystal glasses tinkled as guests raised toasts, their laughter carrying across the manicured lawns.

The gardeners had outdone themselves. Delphiniums stood like blue sentinels along the stone paths, while peonies bobbed their heavy heads in the gentle breeze. Even the hedges had been trimmed into perfect geometric shapes, creating intimate alcoves where ladies gathered to exchange whispered confidences.

Mabel adjusted a centerpiece of lilies as she passed, her fingers brushing the cool petals. She'd risen before dawn to help arrange these displays, combining Clara's vision with her own eye for detail. Now seeing it all come together — the delicate tea cakes arranged on silver stands, the champagne flowing freely, the strings of paper lanterns waiting for dusk – filled her chest with quiet satisfaction.

Clara caught her eye from across the lawn, gesturing subtly for more refreshments. Mabel retrieved a fresh tray of raspberry cordial, navigating between silk skirts and tailored jackets with practiced ease. The crystal glasses barely trembled as she moved, a skill hard-won through months of service.

"The gardens are absolutely magnificent," she heard one lady exclaim to her companion. "The Montagues have truly outdone themselves this year."

Mabel's heart swelled. She'd spent hours helping the gardeners select and arrange each bloom, drawing on memories of her mother's lessons about which flowers complemented each other. The result transformed the already beautiful grounds into something from a fairy tale — though she kept that fanciful thought to herself as she continued her rounds.

A burst of laughter drew Mabel's attention to where Cecilia held court near the rose arbor. Sunlight caught the diamonds at her throat as she tossed her head back, golden curls bouncing with practiced grace. Her admirers clustered close, hanging on her every word as she recounted some amusing tale from London's social season.

Mabel kept to the edges of the gathering, fresh tray balanced carefully as she watched Cecilia gesture with her wine glass. The deep red liquid sloshed dangerously close to the rim with each animated movement. As Cecilia reached the crescendo of her story, her hand swept wide and the glass tilted sharply. Wine cascaded down the front of her cream silk gown, spreading across the delicate fabric in a crimson stain.

The chatter died instantly. Several ladies pressed gloved hands to their mouths in horror. Cecilia's face froze, her perfect composure cracking as she stared at the ruined dress.

Her eyes snapped up, landing on Mabel with laser focus. The mortification in her expression shifted to something harder, more calculated. She yanked at the sodden fabric, displaying the damage to her captive audience.

"This wouldn't have happened if you had been more careful!" Cecilia's voice cracked through the air like a whip. Her manicured finger stabbed toward Mabel in accusation.

Heat flooded Mabel's cheeks as dozens of eyes turned her way. She felt their stares, the barely concealed smirks and raised eyebrows of those eager for scandal. Lady Rowena drifted closer, her face a mask of maternal concern that didn't quite hide the gleam of satisfaction in her eyes.

"My dear, are you quite all right?" Lady Rowena's voice dripped with false sympathy as she patted Cecilia's shoulder, all while watching Mabel squirm under the collective scrutiny of the garden party guests.

Mabel's fingers tightened around the empty serving tray, her knuckles white against the polished silver. The accusation pressed against her chest, threatening to steal her breath. She opened her mouth to defend herself, but no words came.

"Perhaps I might offer a solution." Edward's voice cut through the tension like a fresh breeze. He stepped forward from a nearby cluster of guests, his presence drawing attention away from Mabel. "Miss Downs possesses exceptional skill with lace and needlework. The damage could be transformed into an artistic enhancement."

Heat crept up Mabel's neck at his words. She hadn't expected Edward to remember her background, let alone champion it before the assembled company. His steady gaze met hers, carrying an encouraging warmth that steadied her racing heart.

Cecilia's perfectly shaped mouth twisted, caught between maintaining her accusation and responding to Edward's attention. She smoothed her hands over the wine-stained silk, glancing between Edward's earnest expression and Mabel's flushed face.

"I hardly think—" Cecilia began, but Edward pressed on.

"It will only take a few short moments, I'm sure. What do

you think, Miss Downs?" His voice carried genuine enthusiasm that seemed to capture the interest of nearby guests.

Mabel drew herself up straighter, drawing strength from Edward's confidence in her abilities. She gave a small nod, already envisioning how she might work with the stained fabric.

Cecilia's fingers plucked at the ruined silk, her expression clouded with conflicting desires. To refuse would mean rejecting Edward's suggestion, but accepting meant acknowledging Mabel's skill. After a moment of visible struggle, she lifted her chin.

"Very well," she conceded, though her tone suggested she was granting an enormous favour. "You may attempt to salvage the gown."

Mabel's fingers trembled as she retrieved her sewing kit from her apron pocket. The small leather case held precious needles and threads she'd collected over months of careful saving. She selected a fine silver needle and delicate white thread that would complement the cream silk of Cecilia's gown.

The stain had spread across the skirt in an uneven pattern. Mabel studied it, her artist's eye finding possibility in the damage. From her pocket, she drew a scrap of Brussels lace she'd been working on during quiet moments between duties. The delicate pattern featured trailing vines and tiny flowers — perfect for creating the illusion of intentional design.

She began working quickly, her needle flashing in the afternoon light. The first few stitches anchored the lace firmly to the unstained portion of the skirt. Each subsequent stitch guided the pattern across the wine-marked silk, transforming the angry red stain into shadowing beneath the intricate white overlay.

The chatter around her faded as she worked. Her world narrowed to the push and pull of thread through fabric, the familiar rhythm soothing her rattled nerves. She'd done this countless times before — in the workhouse, at Finch's shop, in stolen moments at the manor. Her hands remembered every lesson her mother had taught her about turning mistakes into opportunities for beauty.

"Extraordinary," someone whispered. "Look how she's incorporating the original beading into the new design."

More guests pressed closer, their jewels catching the sun as they craned their necks for a better view. Mabel kept her eyes on her work, though she felt their scrutiny like physical touch. Her needle danced across the fabric, adding delicate French knots where the stain's edges showed through.

"I've never seen anything quite like it," another voice murmured. "Such clever use of negative space."

The praise warmed Mabel's cheeks, but she didn't let it break her concentration. Each stitch had to be perfect, invisible except where she chose to highlight the pattern. The wine stain became part of the design, lending depth to the cascading floral motif she created.

Lady Rowena's silk skirts rustled as she shifted position. "How... resourceful," she said, her tone suggesting this wasn't entirely a compliment. Through lowered lashes, Mabel caught the slight tightening around Lady Rowena's mouth as more guests gathered to watch the transformation unfold.

Mabel tied off the final stitch and stepped back, her heart fluttering as she surveyed her work. The lace overlay transformed the wine stain into an artistic flourish, as if it had been designed that way from the start. Where moments ago there had been disaster, now delicate flowers bloomed across Cecilia's skirt.

"My word," Lady Fallington breathed, pressing closer. "How cleverly done. Could you create something similar for my daughter's coming out gown?"

Before Mabel could respond, Mrs Gemmaton touched her arm. "And what about a tea dress? I simply must have your work for my garden parties this season."

More ladies crowded around, their earlier disdain forgotten as they examined the intricate needlework. Mabel's fingers still trembled from the pressure of working under their scrutiny, but warmth spread through her chest at their genuine admiration. This was what her mother had always told her — that true craft could bridge any divide.

"Three guineas for the collar piece, wasn't it?" Clara's voice cut through the chatter. "Perhaps we should discuss proper rates for commissioned work." Clara gave Mabel a smile and a wink, and Mabel weakly smiled in thanks. She felt so overwhelmed.

The ladies nodded eagerly, pulling out calling cards and making notes about designs they desired. Mabel accepted each request with careful gratitude, her mind already spinning with patterns she could create.

Through the press of silk skirts and perfumed bodies, Mabel caught sight of Edward standing near the rose arbor. His eyes met hers, warm with pride and something deeper that made her cheeks flush. He gave her a small nod, as if to say 'I knew you could do this.' The quiet confidence in his gaze steadied her, reminding her of all the moments he'd seen her true worth when others looked past her.

COMMISSIONS

*M*abel's fingers moved swiftly across the delicate threads, her needle catching the candlelight as she worked. The manor slept around her, but in her small attic room, she created worlds of beauty in lace. Her back ached from hunching over her work, yet she pressed on, each completed piece bringing her closer to helping Emma and Henry.

Clara had transformed a corner of her sitting room into an impromptu office for Mabel's commissions. Leather-bound books tracked orders and payments, while neat stacks of calling cards reminded them of promised delivery dates. "Let me handle the business side," Clara had insisted, her green eyes sparkling with enthusiasm. "You focus on creating your art."

Now, as Mabel worked on Lady Fallington's intricate collar piece, she wrapped her mother's threadbare coat tighter around her shoulders. The familiar scent of lavender still clung to its fabric, faint but present, like a ghost of Mama's embrace. Her mother's voice seemed to whisper with each stitch: "See how the light catches here? That's where you add the picot edge."

The techniques flowed from her memory – the Brussels

ground stitch her mother had taught her on sunny mornings, the Honiton roses they'd perfected together during long winter evenings. Mabel wove these memories into each piece, adding her own innovations that would have made her Mama proud. Despite her exhaustion, joy bloomed in her as patterns emerged beneath her careful hands.

Clara's organisational skills proved invaluable. She negotiated prices that reflected the true worth of Mabel's craft, ensuring each commission brought in enough to set aside for the orphanage. She arranged delivery schedules and handled correspondence with the ladies, shielding Mabel from the social complexities that might have otherwise overwhelmed her.

In these quiet hours, working by candlelight with her mother's coat around her shoulders, Mabel felt closest to achieving her dreams. Each completed piece meant extra coins for Emma's art supplies or Henry's warm clothes. Her tired fingers moved steadily, transforming thread into delicate flowers and vines, while Clara's meticulously kept ledgers tracked their growing success.

THROUGH THE GRAND windows of the morning room, Mabel noticed Lord Montague watching as yet another carriage arrived bearing ladies eager to commission her lace. His stern expression shifted, not to displeasure as she'd feared, but to the calculating look she'd seen when he discussed railway investments with William.

"Miss Downs." His voice carried across the room as she finished arranging fresh flowers. "A word, if you please."

In his study, Lord Montague sat behind his massive oak desk, fingers steepled beneath his chin. "Your lace work has attracted considerable attention."

"Yes, my lord." Mabel's hands clasped tightly before her.

"I propose an arrangement." He drew out a leather ledger. "The family will take ten percent of your earnings. In exchange, you may continue your enterprise with my explicit approval — something valuable in these circles — alongside all my contacts and services. I realise Clara has already been employing them, but now it would be... all professional."

Mabel's throat tightened. Ten percent would mean less for Emma and Henry. Yet Lord Montague's backing could open doors previously barred to her.

"You may keep the remainder," he continued, "to use as you see fit. Consider it a business partnership of sorts."

The word 'partnership' rang hollow—- she would be merely another investment in his portfolio. But as she thought of Emma's latest letter describing her progress in art classes, and Henry's growing skill with woodwork, Mabel saw the opportunity hidden within this compromise.

"Thank you, my lord. I accept."

He nodded, already turning back to his papers. "Miss Bachman will adjust your duties accordingly. You may go."

Walking back to her attic room, Mabel felt her mother's tablecloth pressed against her skin beneath her dress. Though Lord Montague would profit from her art, she would transform this arrangement into something more — a foundation for her siblings' future, built stitch by careful stitch.

BREAKOUT

Steam rose from the copper pots as Mabel stirred the morning's porridge in the Montague estate's kitchen. The familiar motions brought comfort, even as her thoughts drifted to Emma's latest letter describing a new flower design she'd sketched. The routine of breakfast preparation filled the air with warmth and the quiet clatter of bowls.

The kitchen door burst open. Joan stumbled in with her face ashen. "Typhoid has struck Hampstead!"

The wooden spoon slipped from Mabel's grip, clattering against the floor. Her chest tightened as though bound by iron bands. Emma and Henry's faces flashed before her — their forms waving goodbye at the orphanage gates, their trust in her promise to return.

Blood rushed in her ears as Joan's words echoed through the kitchen. The disease had already claimed three children in the village, she said, and more showed symptoms each day. The orphanage sat at the heart of Hampstead, where the cramped quarters could turn deadly within days.

Mabel's hands trembled as she gripped the edge of the kitchen table. The morning's tasks faded to insignificance against this news. Her siblings, already vulnerable in the orphanage's crowded halls, faced a threat she couldn't shield them from across the miles between them.

The porridge bubbled, forgotten, as Mabel's mind raced through memories of her mother's decline. She'd watched helplessly then as illness stole her mother's breath. Now distance separated her from Emma and Henry when they might need her most.

Mabel fled the kitchen, her footsteps echoing through the servant's corridors as she climbed the narrow stairs to her attic quarters. The tin box lay hidden beneath her thin mattress. Her fingers shook as she pulled it free, counting the coins she'd saved from her lace commissions.

Three pounds, seven shillings. Not enough for a proper doctor if Emma or Henry fell ill, but it might buy medicine or extra blankets. She stuffed the coins into her pocket alongside Emma's latest letter.

The familiar walls of her small room seemed to close in as she grabbed her worn shawl. She couldn't waste time asking permission or explaining her absence. Every hour could mean the difference between life and death at the orphanage. The memory of Mama's final days, the rattle in her chest growing weaker, pushed Mabel toward the door.

"Mabel? What's wrong?" Clara stood in the doorway, her hair half-pinned for the afternoon's garden party. "You look positively ill."

"Nothing, Miss Clara. I just—" Mabel's voice caught as she tried to slip past. "I need to check on my siblings."

"But the Edmontons are arriving any minute. Surely whatever it is can wait until—"

"No." The word came out sharper than Mabel intended. She softened her tone, though her heart hammered. "I'm sorry, Miss Clara, but it can't wait. There's typhoid in Hampstead."

Clara reached for her arm, but Mabel was already moving,

her feet carrying her toward the servant's staircase. The coins jingled in her pocket with each step, a reminder of what little protection she could offer Emma and Henry against the threat bearing down on them.

Mabel's feet pounded against the gravel path, her skirts catching on the manicured hedges of the Montague estate. The morning dew soaked through her worn boots as she cut across the gardens, taking the shortest route to the village rather than following the winding carriage drive.

Market day filled the village square with carts and stalls. Farmers haggled over produce prices while children chased each other between displays of fresh eggs and autumn vegetables. Their laughter pierced through Mabel's panic like discordant notes in a familiar song.

A group of ladies paused their gossip to stare as she rushed past, her hair coming loose from its pins. Their disapproving whispers barely registered. The coins in her pocket bounced against her leg with each step, a constant reminder of what little protection she could offer Emma and Henry.

The coach station sat at the far end of the square, its weathered sign creaking in the breeze. Mabel's lungs burned as she pushed through the crowd.

Her heart thundered in her ears as she approached the station window. The rush of determination flowing through her veins made her fingers tremble as she gripped the wooden counter. Every second spent here meant another moment Emma and Henry faced the threat of typhoid alone. The disease had already claimed three children in Hampstead — she couldn't let it take her siblings too.

EDWARD STOOD AT HIS DESK, reviewing patient records when

Clara burst through the door. Her usually composed demeanour had cracked, revealing genuine distress.

"Mabel's gone. She left for Hampstead." Clara's chest heaved from running. "There's typhoid at the orphanage. Her siblings—"

The quill dropped from Edward's hand, spreading ink across his notes. The image of Mabel's face whenever she spoke of Emma and Henry flashed through his mind. How her eyes lit up reading their letters. How she worked through nights to send them money.

"When did she leave?"

"Just now. She took her savings and ran for the coach station." Clara twisted her hands. "The servants say three children have already died."

Edward's medical training kicked in. Typhoid. The devastating speed of its spread. The horrific toll it took on the young. And Mabel, rushing headlong into its path alone.

"I have to go after her." He yanked his coat from the hook. "She'll need help getting proper care for the children if they're ill."

"But the Edmontons are arriving—"

"Tell Father I had an urgent medical matter." Edward grabbed his medical bag, already moving toward the door. "Which I do."

He strode through the manor's halls, his footsteps echoing against marble. The thought of Mabel facing this crisis alone twisted something in his chest. Their conversations in the clinic, her quiet strength as she helped design spaces for healing –- she'd become more than just another servant. She deserved better than to shoulder this burden by herself.

Edward burst out the front doors and down the steps, startling a footman. The coaching inn lay two miles away. If he rode hard enough, he might catch her before the next coach departed.

THE COACH

The wooden floorboards creaked beneath Mabel's restless feet as she stood in the crowded coaching inn. Her fingers twisted the worn edges of her coin purse, counting and recounting the meagre savings within. Through the din of travelers, she caught fragments of conversation about road conditions and weather, each delay mentioned sending fresh waves of anxiety through her chest.

"Three shillings to Hampstead, miss." The coach driver's gruff voice cut through her thoughts.

Mabel's hands trembled as she sorted the coins. A chill draft swept through the inn's open door, carrying with it a presence that made her pause. The coins clinked against the counter as she felt someone step behind her.

She turned to find Edward there, medical bag in hand, his grey eyes filled with quiet determination. His normally pristine coat showed signs of hasty travel, and his breath came quick from exertion. The sight of him – so clearly having rushed after her – sent her heart into a complicated flutter.

"Miss Downs." His voice was low, meant only for her ears. "You mustn't go alone."

"Master Montague, I—" The words caught in her throat. How could she explain that every moment spent here was another moment her siblings faced danger alone?

"I've brought my medical supplies." He gestured to his bag. "My training could help them. Please, allow me to accompany you."

Edward's presence offered hope, yet the whispers of other travellers reminded her sharply of their different worlds. A gentleman physician and a housemaid — the gossip would spread like wildfire.

But Emma's face floated in her mind, followed by Henry's. Their safety mattered more than society's judgment.

Mabel met Edward's steady gaze and gave a small nod. "Thank you," she whispered, the words carrying both gratitude and concern.

Edward stepped past her to the counter, producing crisp notes from his waistcoat. Her protest died on her lips as he purchased two first-class tickets, his bearing brooking no argument.

The private coach interior gleamed with polished wood and plush velvet seats. Mabel hesitated at the step, her worn boots a stark contrast against the brass fixtures. The last time she'd ridden first class had been years ago, when her father took the family to Brighton for a summer holiday.

"Please." Edward extended his hand to help her up.

Heat crept into her cheeks as she accepted his assistance, careful not to let her fingers linger in his. The leather seat cushion dipped beneath her as she settled by the window.

Edward climbed in after her. The coach door clicked shut, sealing them into an intimate space that made Mabel acutely aware of their solitude. She fixed her gaze on the inn's court-yard through the window, watching stable boys harness fresh horses for their journey.

The horses stamped their feet, and the coach swayed as it

pulled away from the inn, the wheels turning toward Hampstead.

The coach lurched forward, its wheels clattering against the uneven road.

"The last time I traveled this road," Edward said, his voice gentle, "I was chasing after a rather persistent frog that had escaped from my specimen jar."

Despite her worry, Mabel found her lips curving slightly. "Did you catch it?"

"It led me straight into a pond. My father was less than pleased when I arrived home looking like a drowned rat."

The coach hit a bump, and Mabel's hand flew to the window frame to steady herself.

Edward leaned forward, his expression softening. "Your siblings are strong, Miss Downs. Like their sister."

The name — her false name — stung. She turned to watch the passing landscape, letting the cool glass of the window press against her forehead. In her mind, she counted the coins remaining in her purse, calculated the cost of medicines, imagined Emma's face pale with fever or Henry's small frame wracked with chills.

The coach wheels splashed through a puddle, and Mabel caught her reflection in the window — a ghost of herself, overlaid against the grey sky. Edward's presence beside her felt like a lifeline thrown into deep waters, but she couldn't allow herself to grasp it fully. Her siblings needed her clear-headed, focused, ready to face whatever awaited them at the orphanage gates.

She straightened her spine, smoothing her skirts with practiced hands. The motion revealed a loose thread at her cuff — blue, like the forget-me-nots in her mother's garden. She tucked it away carefully, a habit born from years of preserving every scrap of useful material.

CONFESSIONS

The coach rattled over another bump, and Mabel caught Edward stealing another glance at her. His fingers drummed against his medical bag, betraying an unusual nervousness.

"Miss Downs – Mabel." His voice cracked slightly. "I find myself unable to maintain silence any longer."

Mabel's heart skipped as Edward shifted closer, his knee nearly touching hers.

"Over the two years I've known you, which I know is only a short time relatively, but it feels like... I'm rambling, I apologise. But... Your dedication to your siblings, your artistic skill with lace, the way you've faced every challenge with grace — it moves me deeply." Edward's words tumbled out, gaining momentum. "I've never met anyone with such quiet strength."

Heat flooded Mabel's cheeks. The memory of Emma's face at the orphanage window and Henry's worn shoes flashed through her mind.

"Master Montague, I—" She twisted her hands together. "You speak too kindly of a servant."

"Don't." The word came sharp with feeling. "Don't diminish yourself."

Mabel's throat tightened. "There's more you should know. My name isn't Downs." She forced herself to meet his eyes. "It's Fairchild. My father was imprisoned for theft at Hampstead School. Our name is ruined. The shame of it..." She looked down at her worn dress. "You wouldn't want to associate with such disgrace."

"A name doesn't define you," Edward said softly. "Neither does your father's fate."

"I'm an orphan now. My mother's dead and my father—" Her voice caught. "He might as well be. I'm nothing. Just another reason for your father to be angry with you." She looked out the carriage window at the passing countryside. "You deserve someone like Miss Houghton. Someone of your station."

"Cecilia? She's nothing like you. She doesn't understand kindness or hard work. She's never fought for anything in her life."

Tears spilled down Mabel's cheeks before she could stop them. The countryside blurred through the glass. "I just need to save Emma and Henry. That's all that matters now."

"I shouldn't have spoken." Edward's voice softened. "Forgive me."

Mabel shook her head, wiping her eyes with her sleeve. "Don't apologise. It's silly."

"Tell me about them — your siblings." Edward leaned forward. "Emma draws, doesn't she?"

"She loves flowers best." A small smile crept onto Mabel's face despite her tears. "She presses them between paper and tries to capture every detail. And Henry — he has such clever hands. He can whittle the most wonderful little animals."

"We'll save them both." Edward's voice rang with conviction. "I promise you, Mabel. Whatever it takes."

INTO THE FIRE

The coach wheels ground to a halt outside Hampstead Orphanage. The building's grey stone walls loomed before them, more forbidding than she remembered.

No children played in the yard. No voices carried through the windows. Only the whisper of wind through bare branches broke the eerie stillness.

Mabel's boots crunched on gravel as she hurried toward the entrance, Edward matching her pace. Her heart thundered as she pushed open the heavy wooden door. The sharp scent of carbolic soap and boiled cabbage hit her nose, but underneath lay something else —-the sickly-sweet smell of illness.

"This way." Her voice trembled as she led Edward down the dim corridor. Shadows crept along the walls, cast by weak gaslight that did little to dispel the gloom.

Empty beds lined the dormitory, their thin blankets pulled tight. Some still held the impression of small bodies, but the children were gone. Mabel's fingers traced the rough wool of Emma's usual blanket, cold now without her sister's warmth.

"Emma?" She called out, her voice echoing. "Henry?"

No answer came. Only the creak of floorboards under their feet broke the silence.

Room after room revealed the same abandoned scene — scattered toys, half-finished drawings, cups of water gone stale on bedside tables. Each empty space magnified the fear clawing at Mabel's chest.

She paused at the doorway of the infirmary wing, her breath catching. Rows of narrow cots stretched into the shadows. The sharp smell of vinegar and illness grew stronger. Through the gloom, she could make out still forms under blankets, but couldn't tell if any belonged to her siblings.

Mabel burst through the infirmary door, her legs nearly giving way at the sight of Emma. Her sister lay motionless on the narrow cot, skin pale as chalk against the rough sheets. She looked so... different. The last time Mabel had seen her sister, she had been a small thirteen-year-old, but now she was in her mid-teens. She was still small for her age, but her face had matured. Mabel would always know her sister.

Illness, as well as time, had changed Emma. Her golden hair, which had been so bright and full of life, clung damply to her forehead. Mabel dropped to her knees beside the bed, her hands trembling as she reached for Emma's small fingers.

"Emma, I'm here." The words caught in her throat.

Emma's eyes fluttered open, vacant and confused. Mabel squeezed her hand, speaking louder. "Emma, it's Mabel."

No recognition flickered across Emma's face. She stared through Mabel as if she were a stranger, her gaze unfocused and distant. She rubbed against her ear, as Mabel kept saying her name. Mabel's heart cracked when she realised — Emma couldn't hear her voice.

"Oh, my darling." Mabel's tears spilled onto the rough blanket as she stroked Emma's cheek. She forced a smile, though her chest ached with each breath. Emma had always filled their home with laughter and song, even in the darkest times. Now that musical voice might never ring out again.

A crash from the next room drew Mabel's attention. She found Edward kneeling beside Henry's bed, medical bag open on the floor. Henry thrashed against the sheets, his skin burning with fever. Each shallow breath rattled in his chest as he fought for air.

Henry had grown so tall! He must have been taller than Emma now, and maybe even Mabel herself. His lanky limbs sprawled back and forth, and Edward had to fight to bring him under control.

Edward's fingers pressed against Henry's wrist, counting the racing pulse. His usual calm demeanour had vanished, replaced by tight-jawed urgency as he rifled through his supplies.

Mabel hovered helplessly by the doorway, her mind spinning through every remedy their mother had ever taught her for treating illness. Willow bark tea for fever. Cool cloths. Honey and lemon for coughs. But none of it seemed enough in the face of Henry's laboured breathing and Emma's silent confusion.

The infirmary door burst open. Mrs Winters swept in, her face flushed with anger and worry. Two attendants followed close behind, their expressions hardening upon seeing Mabel and Edward.

"What is the meaning of this?" Mrs Winters drew herself up, her voice sharp. "You cannot simply barge in here—"

Mabel's fingers tightened around Henry's hand as she stepped back from the bed. The familiar stern authority in Mrs Winters' face brought back memories of that terrible day she'd left Emma and Henry at the orphanage gates.

Edward straightened from Henry's bedside, his medical bag open beside him. "I am Edward Montague. This boy's fever is dangerously high. He needs immediate treatment."

Mrs Winters' eyes narrowed. "We have our own physician—"

Edward cut in, his tone brooking no argument. "We don't have time for protocols. This child could die within hours without proper care." He turned to the attendants. "I need clean water, fresh linens, and whatever medicines you have in stock. Now!"

The authority in his voice spurred them into action. Even Mrs Winters seemed to deflate slightly, her rigid posture softening as she took in Henry's laboured breathing.

"We've lost three already," Mrs Winters admitted quietly. "The others..." She gestured helplessly toward the rows of occupied beds.

Edward nodded grimly. "Then we have work to do. All of us." He rolled up his sleeves, already moving to check the next patient. "These children need immediate care if they're to survive."

WORKING TOGETHER

$\mathcal{M}$abel watched as Edward transformed before her eyes. Gone was any trace of the gentle medical student — in his place stood a commanding physician. He barked precise instructions to the orphanage staff who had gathered at the commotion, his voice carrying an authority that brooked no argument.

"We need cold compresses immediately. And fetch me clean bandages, carbolic acid, and whatever medicines you have on hand." Edward's fingers pressed against Henry's neck, monitoring his pulse while his other hand checked the boy's temperature. "His fever's dangerously high. We'll need to transfer him to London Hospital – they have better facilities to handle this."

The staff scattered to fulfil his orders. Even Mrs Winters, who normally ruled the orphanage with an iron hand, nodded and hurried to help. Mabel's heart swelled as she watched Edward take control of the situation. For the first time since receiving news of the outbreak, hope flickered within her.

"Mabel, I need your help." Edward called her over while writing quick notes in his journal. "We'll organise the children by severity of symptoms. Can you help assess who needs immediate attention?"

She nodded, grateful for something concrete to do. Together, they moved through the ward, Edward examining each child while Mabel recorded symptoms and arranged for proper care. Her experience managing the household proved invaluable as she coordinated with the staff, ensuring supplies reached where they were needed most.

"The cart for Henry will arrive within the hour," Edward informed her as they prepared clean bedding for another feverish child. "I've arranged for him to be placed under Dr Thompson's care — he's one of the finest physicians in London."

Working alongside Edward felt natural, their movements synchronising as they tended to the sick children. When she anticipated his needs for fresh water or clean cloths, he would give her a quick smile of appreciation. Despite her worry for Emma and Henry, Mabel found strength in their partnership, drawing courage from Edward's steady presence and medical expertise.

THE CART'S wheels rattled against the cobblestones as they made their way to the Hospital. Mabel cradled Emma's head in her lap while Edward monitored Henry's fever. Other children from the orphanage lay bundled in blankets around them, their faces pale against the rough wool.

Emma stirred, her glazed eyes finally focusing on Mabel's face. Recognition flickered across her features — the first sign of awareness since they'd found her. Her small fingers reached out, searching until they found Mabel's hand. The squeeze that followed, though weak, sent relief coursing through Mabel's body.

At the hospital entrance, orderlies rushed forward with

stretchers. Mabel's heart clenched as they lifted Emma and Henry away from her. Edward directed the staff with precise instructions, his voice carrying authority through the chaos.

"These children need immediate attention. Prepare the ward for potential typhoid cases." Edward rolled up his sleeves, ready to assist.

A distinguished gentleman in a black coat approached, his eyes widening at the sight of Edward. "Young Montague? What brings you here?"

"Mr Hornley." Edward nodded in greeting. "We have multiple cases from Hampstead Orphanage requiring urgent care."

Mr Hornley observed as Edward organised the hospital staff, establishing an efficient system for treating the arriving children. His gaze shifted to Mabel, noting her careful assistance with the patients.

"Remarkable work, both of you," Mr Hornley commented, pulling out a small notebook. "Lord Montague should know of this. The hospital board will want to recognise such dedication to public health."

Warmth spread through Mabel's chest. Perhaps this was a sign — a chance for understanding from the Montagues. She watched Mr Hornley scratch out his note, hope rising like a tide within her. The Montagues' support could mean everything for Emma and Henry's care.

CONSPIRACY

*E*dward's fingers traced across the faded ink of hospital admission records, cross-referencing dates and names while monitoring Henry's fever from the corner of his eye. The lamp's glow cast long shadows across the administrative office as he searched for any information that might help Mabel's case.

A letter slipped from between the pages, its seal broken but still bearing the unmistakable crest of the Houghton estate. His heart quickened as he unfolded the paper, revealing correspondence between Mr Ardon and Gerald Houghton, Lady Rowena's late husband. It must have been correspondence from when Mr Houghton had been bed-ridden.

The words jumped from the page: "...the Fairchild plot near Derby holds significant coal deposits... acquisition necessary before surveyor's report becomes public..." Another document detailed payments to Mr Ardon for "services rendered in the matter of Thomas Fairchild's removal."

Edward's hands shook as he laid out the papers across the desk. The dates aligned perfectly — Mr Ardon's arrival at the school, the missing repair funds, his father's accusation. A methodical plan orchestrated to strip Thomas Fairchild of his inherited land through false imprisonment.

Memories of Lady Rowena's calculated smiles at dinner parties took on new meaning. Her persistent visits to the estate, her interest in Derby's development — all part of a wider scheme that had inadvertently destroyed Mabel's family. The realisation struck him like a physical blow: while he had dined in luxury, Mabel had struggled in workhouses because of this conspiracy.

Blood rushed in his ears as he gathered the damning evidence. The names of respected members of society—magistrates, property agents, bankers—all complicit in the scheme to acquire Thomas Fairchild's land through whatever means necessary.

Edward's fingers trembled as he folded the papers, tucking them into the inner pocket of his coat. The evidence pressed against his chest like a stone. His medical training had taught him to diagnose problems methodically, to consider treatments with careful deliberation. This situation required the same measured approach.

Through the office window, he watched Mabel sitting at Emma's bedside, her delicate hands smoothing back the girl's damp hair. Her dedication to her siblings stirred something deep within him. The thought of telling her about Lady Rowena's involvement in her father's imprisonment made his stomach twist.

"Not yet," he whispered to himself. Lady Rowena had proven herself a master of social manipulation. One wrong move could send ripples through society that might harm Mabel further. The woman had already orchestrated the downfall of one Fairchild — Edward wouldn't give her the opportunity to target another.

He pulled out his pocket watch, running his thumb over its polished surface. Time ticked steadily forward while his mind raced through possibilities. The evidence needed verification, witnesses would have to be found, and most importantly, Mabel's siblings needed to recover their health before any action could be taken.

Edward straightened his shoulders and squared his jaw. He had chosen medicine to help those in need, to fight against suffering and injustice. This battle would require different weapons than his medical bag, but the principle remained the same. He would see Thomas Fairchild freed and his family's name restored, no matter the cost to his own social standing.

EVERYTHING TO ME

The coach rattled along the northern road toward Derbyshire. Mabel pressed her forehead against the window, watching raindrops chase each other across the glass. Her heart felt stretched between two points — behind her in Hampstead where Emma and Henry lay in hospital beds, and ahead where duty called her back to the estate.

"Dr Thompson has treated hundreds of fever cases." Edward's voice cut through her worried thoughts. "He pioneered a cooling technique that's saved countless lives."

"Emma couldn't hear me when I spoke to her." Mabel's fingers twisted in her lap. "And Henry's fever was so high."

"The deafness may be temporary. Many patients recover their hearing once the fever breaks." Edward leaned forward, his grey eyes intent. "I've seen it myself during my training. And if she doesn't, we'll learn other ways to communicate with her."

The coach hit a rough patch, jostling them both. Edward steadied himself with a hand against the carriage wall. "We'll return to check on them in two days' time. I've arranged everything with Dr Thompson."

Mabel nodded, trying to draw strength from his certainty. "I don't know how to thank you properly. For everything — the hospital, Dr Thompson, even coming with me in the first place."

"You don't need to thank me." Edward's voice softened. "Any decent person would help children in need."

"But most decent people wouldn't risk their reputation or position to do it." Mabel met his gaze. "You did both without hesitation."

A flush crept up Edward's neck. "I did what was right. Nothing more."

"It was everything to us." Mabel's voice caught. "To me."

ACCUSED

The Montague estate emerged through the mist, its grand facade a stark reminder of the world Mabel had fled from days ago. The familiar gardens and manicured lawns felt foreign now, transformed by her desperate journey to Hampstead and the weight of Emma and Henry's illness that still pressed upon her heart.

Edward's boots crunched on the gravel drive as he helped Mabel down from the coach. His shoulders were set with purpose, but Mabel caught the slight tremor in his hands as he released hers. The morning air hung heavy with dew and unspoken worries.

The great oak doors loomed before them, polished to a shine that reflected their approaching figures. Edward paused, his hand on the brass handle. "Let me speak first."

Inside, the grand hall stretched out in elegant splendour, morning light streaming through tall windows to illuminate the Persian carpets and oil paintings. But the beauty paled before the sight of Lord Montague standing at the foot of the main staircase.

He cut an imposing figure against the marble steps, his

morning coat pristine, his face carved from stone. Papers clutched in one hand bore the crumpled evidence of his grip. Behind him, a parlour maid froze in the act of arranging flowers, her eyes wide at the brewing storm.

"What were you thinking, Edward?" Lord Montague's voice thundered through the hall, echoing off the high ceiling. "Abandoning your responsibilities, fleeing like a common vagrant? And for what? To play doctor to orphans?" His knuckles whitened around the papers. "The Edmontons were here. Lady Cecilia was left waiting, expecting for you to turn up!"

"Father, I —"

"Do not speak to me as such, boy. I am *sir* to you, especially in this moment."

Edward's jaw tightened, and he nodded mechanically. "Yes, sir."

Mabel's heart sank as Lady Rowena's silk skirts rustled from behind a marble column. She glided forward like a cat preparing to pounce, her burgundy gown catching the morning light. The corners of her mouth lifted in a practiced smile that never reached her eyes.

"My dear Lord Montague." Lady Rowena's voice floated through the hall, sweet as poisoned honey. "I fear the situation is far graver than mere youthful impetuosity." She positioned herself beside Lord Montague, her fingers trailing along the bannister. "We must consider the... calculated nature of these events."

The words sliced through the air between them. "Your son, with his generous heart, has fallen prey to the oldest of snares." Lady Rowena's gaze fixed on Mabel, sharp as a needle. "A servant girl, playing on his sympathies with tales of sick children. How convenient that her 'emergency' required him to abandon his obligations to Cecilia. To travel, unchaperoned, for days." Her lips curled. "One might almost admire such... calculated feminine wiles."

The accusation burned through Mabel's chest like fire. She stepped forward, her fingers curling into fists at her sides. The polished floor beneath her feet felt as unstable as ice, but she forced herself to move.

"My siblings were dying." Mabel's voice wavered but didn't break. She lifted her chin, meeting Lord Montague's stern gaze. "I have never sought to manipulate anyone. I only wished to help my brother and sister." Her words rang through the hall, clear and true. "They are all I have left in this world, and I had to try to save them."

Lord Montague's stern expression softened, almost imperceptibly. He shifted his weight, his fingers loosening their grip on the crumpled papers. "A sister and brother, you say?" His voice carried a note of understanding that made Mabel's heart leap. "And their condition?"

"Henry's fever has broken, my lord. The doctors believe he will recover." Mabel's voice steadied as she spoke of her siblings. "Emma... Emma's hearing was affected, but she lives."

Lord Montague nodded slowly, his eyes distant as if remembering something from long ago. The morning light caught the silver in his hair, and for a moment, Mabel glimpsed the father beneath the lord.

"But there's more!" Lady Rowena's voice cut through the moment like a knife. She stepped forward, pulling something from behind the marble column. Mabel's breath caught in her throat as Lady Rowena unfurled her mother's wedding tablecloth with a dramatic flourish.

Mabel's heart plummeted at the sight of her mother's wedding tablecloth in Lady Rowena's grasp. In her desperate rush to reach Emma and Henry, Mabel had left it behind in her attic room, forgotten in that moment of panic.

Lady Rowena's fingers traced the edge of the tablecloth with deliberate slowness. "Such exquisite work," she mused, her eyes never leaving Mabel's face. "Far too fine for a mere servant to possess. One might wonder how you acquired such a valuable piece."

The urge to snatch the tablecloth from Lady Rowena's hands nearly overwhelmed Mabel, but she forced herself to remain still. That precious piece of her mother's life, her family's history, now dangled like evidence of some imagined crime.

"It was my mother's," Mabel managed to say, her voice barely above a whisper. "She made it for her wedding day." The words felt inadequate to convey the hours of love and dedication woven into each pattern, the memories contained in every stitch.

Lady Rowena's smile sharpened. "How convenient. And I suppose you can prove this claim?"

The delicate lace caught the sunlight streaming through the tall windows, its intricate patterns casting ethereal shadows across the polished floor. The familiar peonies and forget-me-nots that Mary had woven with such care seemed to dance in the morning light.

"You see this?" Lady Rowena's voice rang with triumph through the grand hall. "Mabel stole this from Cecilia's trousseau collection. Your precious lace is nothing but deceit."

Heat rushed to Mabel's cheeks as the accusation hung in the air. Her heart hammered against her ribs as memories of her mother flooded back — Mary bent over the lace table, teaching Mabel the delicate stitches, working through the night to complete this wedding gift that had graced their table through both joy and sorrow.

"It's not true! This was my mother's!" The words burst from Mabel's lips, raw with desperation. She took a step toward the tablecloth, her fingers aching to touch the familiar patterns, to reclaim this piece of her mother's legacy. But Lady Rowena quickly passed it to Lord Montague.

Lord Montague's took the tablecloth gently. The morning light caught the silver threads, and for a moment, his expression softened – perhaps recognising the skill in each stitch. But as his gaze lifted to meet Mabel's, that fleeting warmth vanished.

"These patterns." His voice carried the weight of judgment. "They match exactly the style commissioned for the Houghton collection."

The grand hall seemed to shrink around Mabel, pressing in with accusations. Her throat tightened as Lord Montague's shoulders stiffened, his earlier moment of paternal understanding replaced by the rigid posture of aristocratic duty.

"They're the same because I made the Houghton collection! I based it off my mother's—"

"To think we welcomed you into our home." His words cut through the air. "Trusted you with our hospitality." Each syllable dropped like stones, building a wall between them.

Lady Rowena circled closer. Her smile stretched wider, satisfaction gleaming in her eyes as she watched Mabel's world crumble. She positioned herself beside Lord Montague, one gloved hand resting possessively on the tablecloth.

"Such a shame." Lady Rowena's voice dripped with false sympathy. "One hopes to find gratitude in those we lift from... unfortunate circumstances." Her gaze swept over Mabel's simple dress. "Instead, we discover theft and manipulation."

Lady Rowena's triumph radiated through the hall. The woman's calculated pleasure in Mabel's distress was unmistakable — each word another thread in the web she'd spun, each gesture a reminder of the social gulf between them.

The grand hall's silence pressed against Mabel's ears like cotton wool, muffling everything except the thundering of her heart. Her fingers trembled at her sides as she stared at her mother's tablecloth.

Edward stepped forward. "This is wrong, Father! We should hear Mabel's side." His voice carried a conviction, cutting through the suffocating atmosphere. "You cannot possibly believe—"

"Edward." Lady Rowena's voice sliced through his protest like a blade. Her eyes narrowed, fixing him with a look that could freeze water. "This is not the time to defend her." She adjusted her burgundy skirts with deliberate precision, each movement calculated. "Consider the implications her presence has on our reputation."

Mabel watched the exchange, her throat tight with unshed tears. The manipulation hanging thick in the air was almost visible — Lady Rowena orchestrating each moment like a conductor before her orchestra. Every word, every gesture served to remind the Montagues of their position, their duty to uphold society's rigid expectations.

The familiar patterns of her mother's tablecloth seemed to mock her now, transformed from comfort into condemnation by Lady Rowena's skilled hands. Mabel felt the walls of propriety and class closing in, leaving her no space to defend herself or her family's honour.

DISMISSAL

*M*abel's fingers twisted in her apron as Lord Montague's study closed in around her. The afternoon light streaming through tall windows did nothing to warm the chill that had settled in her bones. Miss Bachman stood rigid beside the massive oak desk, her face carved from stone.

"These accusations are quite serious." Lord Montague's voice filled the space between them. He held Mary's tablecloth like evidence at a trial, each delicate stitch now a mark against her. "Theft, deception, manipulation of my son's good nature."

"My lord, please." Mabel's voice cracked. She had waited dutifully as protocol was followed and Miss Bachman had been called. She knew that this was her final chance. "That tablecloth was my mother's wedding gift. Every pattern tells our family's story." The words tumbled out, desperate to make them understand. "The peonies were from her garden, the forget-me-nots—"

"Enough." Miss Bachman's sharp tone cut through the air. "A proper servant knows her place."

"I have been nothing but honest in my work here." Mabel's

chest tightened as she fought to keep her composure. "Ask anyone about my character—"

Lord Montague's hand slammed against his desk. "Your character?" His eyes narrowed. "You entered this household under a false name."

"Father, you must listen." Edward stepped forward from the shadows near the door. "Mabel had no choice—"

"Be silent, Edward." Lord Montague's voice carried the experience of years of command. "You've been thoroughly deceived by this... this girl's artifice."

Clara rushed to Mabel's side. "But Uncle, Mabel has shown nothing but dedication and skill. Her lace work alone—"

"Both of you." Lord Montague rose from his chair. "You are young and easily swayed by sob stories and pretty faces. Leave us."

Their protests died under the Lord Montague's stern gaze.

The choice crystallised in her mind. She could fight — explain the truth about her father's imprisonment, reveal the depth of her feelings for Edward — but the cost would be too great. Edward's medical work, his dreams of helping others, his position in society — she couldn't bear to see it all crumble because of her.

"My lord." Mabel's voice remained steady despite the tremor in her heart. "I accept my dismissal. Thank you for the opportunities you've provided." She curtsied, keeping her eyes lowered to hide the tears threatening to spill.

In her attic room, Mabel packed her few belongings into a small bundle — the tin box containing Emma's drawings, Henry's wooden top, and the notebook filled with lace patterns. Each item felt heavier than the last.

The grand hallway echoed with her footsteps as she walked toward the entrance. Voices drifted from the drawing room — Lady Rowena's triumphant tone, the clink of teacups, scattered laughter. Mabel's throat tightened at the sound of Edward's absence.

Just before she reached the door, a soft rustle of skirts caught her attention. Clara appeared from the shadows of the morning room, her face etched with concern.

"Mabel, wait." Clara pressed a small velvet pouch into her hands. The weight of coins shifted inside. "Take this. It's not much, but it should help you start again."

"Miss Clara, I couldn't possibly—"

"Please." Clara's fingers wrapped around Mabel's, ensuring she couldn't refuse. "You've been more than a lady's maid to me. You've been a friend."

Warmth bloomed in Mabel, cutting through the chill of her circumstances. The coins represented more than money — they were proof that someone believed in her, understood her worth beyond her station.

"And Emma..." Clara's voice softened as she squeezed Mabel's hands. "I've already sent word to the hospital. As soon as she's well enough to travel, both she and Henry will join you. Just make sure to send me your new address."

Mabel's breath caught in her throat. "But how—"

"Dr Thompson is an old friend of our family. He'll ensure they're properly cared for until they can be moved." Clara's green eyes sparkled with determination. "I won't see your family separated again, not after everything you've been through."

The weight that had pressed against Mabel's chest since Lady Rowena's accusations lifted slightly. Emma and Henry would be with her. Whatever challenges lay ahead, they would face them together.

"I don't know how to thank you." Mabel's voice wavered as she clutched the velvet pouch.

"You already have, through your friendship." Clara pulled Mabel into a tight embrace, her usual propriety forgotten.

"Promise me you'll be careful. I'll find ways to send word when I can. I'm returning to Brighton next month, but I'll find ways to help."

Mabel hugged her back fiercely, memorising the lavender scent of Clara's dress and the warmth of true friendship. "I promise. And you must be careful too. Lady Rowena..."

"Has no power over me," Clara finished with quiet conviction. "Now go, before anyone sees us."

They separated reluctantly, sharing one final look of understanding. Clara's kindness had given Mabel something beyond mere coins — she had given her hope.

FREEDOM

*M*abel climbed the narrow stairs to her newly rented attic apartment in Derby, each step creaking under her feet. The space stretched before her — small but filled with possibility. A single window cast long shadows across the wooden floor, dust motes dancing in the afternoon light.

She placed her bundle on a rickety table. Her fingers traced the rough windowsill. Below, Derby's streets pulsed with life — cart wheels rattling over cobblestones, merchants calling their wares, children playing between market stalls. Different from Hampstead's quiet lanes, but somehow promising in its busy energy.

Mabel unpacked her few possessions, arranging them with careful precision. Her lace-making tools found their place near the window where light would be strongest. A small bed tucked into the corner would do until she could afford proper furniture for Emma and Henry.

Henry and Emma. Their faces filled her mind — Henry's serious expression when concentrating on a task, Emma's bright eyes lighting up upon seeing the flowers. Soon they would be here, their laughter echoing off these walls, their presence transforming this empty space into something more.

She pictured Emma's gasp of delight upon seeing the window's view of chimney tops and distant hills. Henry would claim the corner near the fireplace, perhaps setting up a small workbench for his wooden crafts. Their joy at being together again would chase away the apartment's current emptiness.

The thought strengthened her resolve. With Clara's help ensuring their safe transport from the hospital, and the coins providing a modest start, Mabel could build something here. Not the cottage they'd lost, but something new — a home created from determination and love rather than inherited comfort.

The attic apartment, though sparce, held patches of sunlight that warmed the wooden floors. She scattered the petals along the windowsill, their faded colors catching the light like fragments of stained glass.

The scents of market day drifted up through the window — fresh bread, horses, and coal smoke. Different from Hampstead's gentle village air, but alive with possibility. She hung a length of simple muslin as a curtain, the fabric dancing in the breeze.

Her mother's lessons echoed in her mind as she arranged her workspace near the window. Mama had always said good light was a lacemaker's first tool. The wooden table, though scratched, felt solid beneath her fingers. She placed her bobbins in precise rows, each one carrying memories of hours spent learning at her mother's side.

The space slowly transformed under her touch. A bundle of lavender tied with twine hung from a nail, its subtle fragrance masking the mustiness of the attic. She'd found wild roses growing against a weathered fence, their petals now scattered across her pillow. Even the rough walls seemed softer in the evening light, embracing rather than confining.

The apartment might be humble, but it was hers. No one could dictate her movements here or judge her work. She could create without fear of criticism, experiment with new patterns that had been forming in her mind. For the first time since leaving the Montague estate, Mabel felt her shoulders relax, her breathing ease. This space, however small, offered freedom.

EDWARD'S PROMISE

*E*dward stood in his father's study, the familiar scent of leather-bound books and pipe tobacco doing nothing to ease the tension between them. Lord Nathaniel's fingers drummed against the mahogany desk.

"The Edinburgh Medical Society has specifically requested your attendance." His father's voice carried the weight of generations of Montague authority. "Their surgical program is unmatched in all of Britain."

"Father, I have responsibilities here. The clinic—"

"The clinic can wait." Lord Nathaniel's hand sliced through the air. "You've spent enough time playing country doctor. If you are going to stay committed to this apparent crusade of yours, it's time you pursued proper medical advancement."

Edward's jaw clenched. The real meaning hung unspoken between them—distance from Mabel Fairchild and her unfortunate circumstances.

"The carriage leaves tomorrow morning." His father shuffled papers, a clear dismissal. "Pack what you need for six months."

In his chambers, Edward folded his medical journals and instruments with mechanical precision. Through the window, late afternoon sun painted the Derbyshire hills in shades of amber. Somewhere in those hills, Mabel worked at her lace, building a new life despite every obstacle thrown in her path.

His fingers traced the edge of a document hidden between his journals — the damning evidence he'd discovered at the hospital. The pages whispered of corruption, of Lady Rowena's schemes, of Thomas Fairchild's stolen years.

Edward closed his trunk with a sharp click. The weight of privilege sat heavy on his shoulders as he gazed across the estate grounds one final time. Though his father might send him away, no distance could erase what he'd witnessed — Mabel's strength during the typhoid crisis, her unwavering dedication to her siblings, the quiet dignity with which she faced every challenge.

He pressed his palm against the cool windowpane. "I will return," he whispered, though no one could hear. "And I will make this right."

REUNION

*M*abel paced the cobblestones, her eyes fixed on the corner where Dr. Thompson's carriage would appear. The morning fog clung to Derby's buildings, wrapping the street in gray shadows. Her heart thundered with each passing cart and carriage.

A dark shape emerged through the mist. The carriage wheels clattered to a stop.

Emma burst out first, her face flushed with excitement. Henry followed, steadier on his feet than when Mabel had last seen him at the hospital. Their clothes, fresh and clean, spoke of Clara's careful attention to detail.

Mabel's legs gave way. She dropped to her knees as Emma and Henry crashed into her arms. The cobblestones pressed hard against her knees, but she barely noticed. Emma's familiar scent of lavender soap filled her nose. Henry's thin arms wrapped around her neck with surprising strength.

"Mabel, Mabel, Mabel," Emma's voice came out too loud. Her hearing was still gone. Tears streaked down Emma's cheeks as she pressed her face into Mabel's shoulder.

Henry didn't speak. His fingers clutched Mabel's dress, his

body trembling with quiet sobs. Mabel pulled them both closer, her own tears falling freely. The three of them knelt there in the street, clinging to each other as if letting go might make the moment disappear.

Dr Thompson stepped down from his carriage, a letter from Clara visible in his coat pocket. But Mabel barely registered his presence. Her world had narrowed to the feeling of Emma's hair against her cheek and Henry's heartbeat against her chest. They were here. They were safe. They were together.

The morning fog lifted around them, revealing a clear autumn day. But Mabel remained on her knees, holding her siblings, memorising the weight of them in her arms. After so many years of separation, letters, and worry, the simple act of embracing them felt like coming home.

Mabel rose from the cobblestones, keeping one arm around each sibling. Her eyes brimmed with fresh tears as she faced Dr Thompson.

"Thank you. I can't begin to express my gratitude for bringing them to me."

Dr Thompson's kind eyes crinkled at the corners. "Emma's hearing hasn't returned. The fever took that from her, I'm afraid." He glanced at Emma, who watched their lips moving with intense concentration. "It will require patience and new ways of communicating. All of you will need to adapt."

Henry squeezed Mabel's hand, and she squeezed back.

"The three of you will develop your own language of gestures and signs. Emma's other senses will grow stronger to compensate." Dr Thompson's smile deepened. "But I've seen how you care for them. Your dedication during the outbreak showed me everything I needed to know about your character."

Mabel's throat tightened. "You heard about the estate?"

"Indeed. That business with the tablecloth." He shook his head. "No thief would have worked through the night caring for sick children as you did. No deceiver would have risked exposure to typhoid to save others. Your actions speak far louder than any accusations."

Emma tugged at Mabel's sleeve, her face questioning. Mabel pulled her close, pressing a kiss to her forehead. They would find their way together, as they always had.

Dr Thompson tipped his hat and climbed back into his carriage. The wheels clattered against the cobblestones as he disappeared around the corner, leaving Mabel with her arms still wrapped around Emma and Henry.

"Come," Mabel guided them toward her building. "Our home is just up these stairs."

Emma's eyes widened at the narrow staircase, while Henry gripped the railing. Their footsteps echoed in the dim passageway as they climbed to the attic. Mabel's hand trembled slightly as she turned the key in the lock.

Sunlight streamed through the muslin curtains, casting a gentle glow across the small room. Emma rushed to the window seat where Mabel's lace pillows rested, running her fingers over the delicate patterns. Henry stood in the centre, taking in the dried flowers hanging from the rafters and the neat pile of wood scraps Mabel had collected for his carving.

"I know it's not much," Mabel started, but Emma spun around, her face radiant. She pointed to the flowers, then to herself, making the connection to her pressed flower collection from before. Henry had already discovered the wooden box containing his old top and their father's poetry book.

Mabel watched as they explored every corner — Emma discovering the shelf where Mabel had arranged her drawing supplies, Henry examining the small table near the window that would serve as his workbench. Their excitement filled the modest space with life and warmth that had been missing since Mabel first arrived.

Three cups sat ready on the small table, alongside a pot of tea and the last of Clara's gifted biscuits. Mabel had laid out this welcome for days, replacing the tea each morning, waiting for this moment. Now, as she poured the fresh brew, her hands steadied. Emma settled beside her, leaning against her shoulder, while Henry claimed the wooden stool Mabel had carefully cushioned for him.

The steam rose from their cups, curling in the sunlight. For the first time since their mother's death, the three Fairchilds sat together, whole again despite everything that had tried to break them apart.

A NEW NORMAL

Mabel's fingers moved through the familiar motions as dawn broke over Derby. The lace pattern beneath her hands spoke of winter roses surviving frost, their delicate petals rendered in thread that caught the early light. She'd developed this design after watching Emma press flowers between pages, preserving their beauty even as they grew fragile.

Each day brought new challenges. Her shoulders ached from hunching over the work table, and her eyes strained in the dim morning hours. But she refused to let exhaustion dull the precision of her stitches. Her mother's voice echoed in her memory — "The strength lies in the details, dear one."

Emma sat across from her, sketching flowers with swift, sure strokes. Their new language flowed between them — Emma's fingers dancing through the air to ask about breakfast, Mabel's hands shaping responses about toast and jam. Henry had created a wooden board where they posted common signs, each one carefully illustrated by Emma.

"More tea?" Mabel's hands formed the question.

Emma nodded, her smile bright as she demonstrated their

newest gesture for "delicious" — fingers brushing lips then spreading outward like petals opening.

Henry sat at his small workbench, sawdust coating his apron. He'd taken to carving specialised tools for Mabel's lace-work, each one tested and refined until it matched her needs perfectly. His hands moved in their shared language: "The new bobbin works better?"

Mabel held up her latest piece, where the thread tension showed the improvement. Their mother's techniques formed the foundation, but Mabel had begun incorporating Emma's flower studies and Henry's practical innovations. Each piece told their story — traditional patterns flowing into new forms, strength and beauty intertwined.

MABEL GATHERED her latest lace pieces into a leather portfolio, each one nestled between sheets of tissue paper. The winter roses design had sparked interest among local ladies, and she needed a way to reach them without drawing Lady Rowena's attention.

The bell above Mr Bennett's shop door chimed as she entered. Morning light streamed through the windows, catching the dust motes dancing above shelves of ribbons and buttons. Mr Bennett looked up from his ledger, his round spectacles catching the gleam.

"Ah, Miss Fairchild. Your timing is perfect." He gestured to an empty display case near the window. "Just cleared this space yesterday."

Mabel set her portfolio on the counter, careful not to disturb the neat stacks of paper and thread. "Are you certain about this, Mr Bennett?"

"Never been more certain of anything." He opened the portfolio with reverent hands. "These pieces deserve to be seen.

Though perhaps not under the Fairchild name, given recent... circumstances."

"What do you suggest?"

Mr Bennett pulled out a small card he'd prepared. In elegant script, it read 'M. Hampstead Lace.' "Simple, dignified. Speaks of quality without drawing unwanted attention."

Mabel traced the letters with her finger. The name honoured her origins without exposing her family to further scrutiny. "It's perfect."

"We'll display them properly." Mr Bennett moved to the case, arranging the winter rose collar on black velvet. "Let the work speak for itself."

The lace caught the light, each stitch precise and purposeful. Mabel watched as Mr Bennett positioned her other pieces — a delicate cuff, a handkerchief border, a small tablecloth. Under his careful arrangement, they transformed from mere items into works of art.

"There." He stepped back, satisfied. "Now we wait for the right eyes to find them."

CLEAR MEMORY

$\mathcal{E}$dward stared at the anatomical diagrams pinned across his Edinburgh quarters, but his mind wandered to Derby. The sharp lines of arteries and veins blurred into patterns of lace. He pushed back from his desk, rubbing his temples.

"Montague, you're missing Knox's demonstration." His colleague Phillips stuck his head through the doorway. "Fascinating dissection of the—"

"Can't. Need to finish these case studies." Edward waved him off, though the papers before him remained untouched.

The clock struck three. Usually by this hour, he'd be deep in discussion with Professor Hamilton about surgical techniques. Instead, he found himself sketching clinic layouts in his margins, adding windows where Mabel had suggested better light would aid recovery.

Her laugh echoed in his memory — that day she'd caught him drawing stick figures of patients in his medical journal. "Perhaps I should teach you proper illustration," she'd teased, her eyes bright with mischief.

Edward pushed away from his desk and paced the room.

The surgical society had invited him to another evening of port and professional connections. He'd declined, preferring solitude to forced pleasantries.

"Distraction leads to poor technique," Professor Hamilton often warned. But Edward's finest work had come during those days at the orphanage, Mabel steady at his side as they fought to save her brother. Her practical wisdom had enhanced his medical knowledge, creating something greater than either could achieve alone.

He pulled out his journal, running his fingers over the dried flowers pressed between its pages — Emma's artwork, preserved from the clinic plans. The petals had faded, like his father's reasons for sending him away. But his resolve had only strengthened.

"I'll find you," he whispered to the empty room. "We'll build that clinic together, whatever it takes."

The Edinburgh bells tolled across the city. Edward turned back to his studies, but Mabel's face remained clear in his mind — her determination, her grace under pressure, her ability to create beauty even in darkness.

INDEPENDENCE

*M*abel arranged her teaching space in the back room of the shop, where light pooled through the window onto a circular table. Mr Bennett had been gracious enough to lend the space to her, and her lace was doing very well for the business.

Six women gathered around her, their faces bright with anticipation. Eleanor Cooper, a baker's wife with quick fingers, sat closest, while Mary-Beth from the millinery shop leaned forward, memorising each movement of Mabel's hands.

"The trick lies in the tension," Mabel demonstrated, her bobbins dancing. "Too tight, and the pattern becomes rigid. Too loose, and it loses shape entirely."

The women's needles clicked in harmony as they practiced. Nancy Warner, whose husband had lost his job at the mill, showed particular promise. Her determination reminded Mabel of herself in those early days at Finch's shop.

"Like this?" Nancy held up her work, a small flower taking shape.

"Exactly." Mabel adjusted Nancy's grip slightly. "You have a natural touch."

Emma moved among the women, distributing tea in mismatched cups. The room filled with quiet conversation and occasional laughter — a sound that had once seemed lost to them forever.

"My grandmother made lace," Alice Thatcher shared, her voice soft with memory. "But she never had the chance to teach me before she passed."

"Now you'll carry on her legacy," Mabel replied, watching Alice's fingers grow more confident with each stitch.

The afternoon light cast long shadows across their work as the women mastered basic patterns. Mabel observed their progress with quiet joy, seeing echoes of her mother's teachings in her own instructions. Her mother's patience, her attention to detail, her belief in creating beauty even in darkness — all lived on in this circle of women.

Each completed piece represented more than mere craft. Eleanor's lace would help pay for her son's apprenticeship. Nancy's work meant food on her table. Alice's designs would add beauty to her church's altar cloths. Together, they wove not just threads but hope, dignity, and independence into every pattern.

PROOF OF INNOCENCE

*E*dward stepped into the solicitor's office on Fleet Street, his medical bag still by his side despite having completed his Edinburgh studies just days ago. The office smelled of leather-bound books and pipe tobacco, a scent that reminded him of his father's study. But unlike the cold formality of home, this place held the promise of justice.

"Mr Grayson?" Edward placed his research on the polished desk. "I believe there's been a grave miscarriage of justice regarding a schoolmaster in Hampstead."

The solicitor adjusted his spectacles, his weathered hands moving through the papers Edward had gathered. Each document showed a different piece of the puzzle — letters between Ardon and the late Gerald Houghton, property deeds, and financial records Edward had discovered during the typhoid outbreak.

"Most interesting." Grayson's finger traced a line of signatures. "These payment records... they don't align with the school's regular accounts."

"Precisely." Edward leaned forward. "The funds Mr Fairchild allegedly stole — they were never meant for school repairs."

Grayson pulled out additional documents from his own files. "I handled several property disputes in Derbyshire during that period. The Houghton estate was particularly aggressive in acquiring land with potential coal deposits."

Together, they spread the papers across the desk. Grayson produced a map of Derbyshire, marking locations where the Houghtons had expanded their mining operations. A small plot, previously owned by the Fairchild family, sat directly between two productive mines.

"Here." Grayson circled the location. "Your Mr Ardon served as more than just a schoolmaster. He was Gerald Houghton's agent in several property acquisitions. The timing of Thomas Fairchild's arrest coincides perfectly with Lady Rowena's husband's push to consolidate these mining interests."

Edward's jaw tightened as he recognised Lady Rowena's familiar signature on documents dated just weeks before Thomas' arrest. The evidence of collaboration between her and Ardon lay bare before them, each piece fitting together like a macabre puzzle.

Grayson rifled through another stack of documents, his eyes widening. He pulled out a yellowed letter, its edges worn but the ink still clear. "Look at this, Mr Montague."

Edward's pulse quickened as he read. If you knew what you were looking for, this letter detailed Ardon's careful manipulation of the school's financial records — fabricated receipts, altered dates, and deliberately misplaced documents that had sealed Thomas' fate.

"This proves it." Edward slammed a finger onto the damning evidence. "Ardon created a perfect illusion of embezzlement while the funds were actually being funnelled through multiple accounts to purchase Thomas' inherited land."

More papers emerged — a trail of correspondence between Ardon and Gerald Houghton's solicitors, each piece revealing the calculated destruction of an innocent man's life. Edward thought of Mabel's unwavering faith in her father's innocence, her determination to keep her family together despite impossible odds. Her strength had awakened something in him — a desire to fight against the injustices his own class too often inflicted on others.

"We must act quickly." Grayson pulled out fresh paper, his pen scratching across the surface. "I'll draft a petition for immediate release. The evidence is irrefutable — the court cannot ignore such a clear miscarriage of justice. We cannot get Mr Fairchild the six years he has lost, but we can save his next nine!"

Edward watched as Grayson crafted the legal arguments, each paragraph building a fortress of truth around Thomas' innocence. His mind wandered to the moment Thomas would walk free, imagining the joy on Mabel's face when her father returned to her and her siblings. The thought filled him with renewed purpose.

"The Home Secretary must see this immediately." Grayson's pen flew across the page. "With evidence this compelling, we can demand an expedited review. No man should spend another day in prison when proof of his innocence exists."

RELEASE

*E*dward stood in the crisp morning air outside Maidstone Prison's iron gates. The weathered stone walls cast long shadows across the cobblestones, a stark reminder of the unjust years they had contained an innocent man. Beside him, Grayson clutched the papers that proved Thomas Fairchild's innocence.

The heavy gates creaked open. Thomas Fairchild emerged, blinking in the bright sunlight. His once-dark hair had turned completely grey, his frame gaunt beneath clothes that hung loose on his shoulders. Yet he carried himself with unmistakable dignity, his eyes — the same shade as Mabel's —-scanning the street with quiet intensity.

Edward's chest tightened as he observed the man's careful movements. Though prison had taken its toll on Thomas' body, it hadn't broken his spirit. The way he held his head high, the careful way he placed each foot forward — these small gestures spoke of resilience that reminded Edward so much of Mabel.

Grayson stepped forward, extending his hand. "Mr Fairchild, I'm Richard Grayson. This is Edward Montague. He's the one that brought your case to my attention. We've uncovered evidence that proves your innocence in the matter of the school funds."

Thomas' weathered hands trembled slightly as he accepted the handshake. His voice, when it came, carried the hoarseness of long disuse. "My children — are they well?"

The simple question, devoid of bitterness or self-pity, struck Edward deeply. Here was a man whose first thought upon regaining freedom was for his family's welfare. Pride swelled in Edward's chest, knowing he had played a part in bringing justice to this good man.

Thomas' hands clasped together, his knuckles white with emotion. "I cannot express my gratitude enough, Mr Montague, Mr Grayson. Your efforts have given me back my freedom, but there is only one thing that matters now — finding my family."

Edward watched as Thomas' eyes filled with unshed tears, yet his voice remained steady. "Every night in that cell, I would close my eyes and see them. Mabel, teaching Emma to write her letters at the kitchen table. Henry, always trailing after his sisters with that wooden top spinning in his hands."

The morning sun caught the silver in Thomas' hair as he continued, each word carrying the pain of years of separation. "Mabel had such patience with them both. She'd help Emma practice her reading while keeping Henry entertained with little games. Just like her mother, that girl."

Thomas pulled a worn piece of paper from his jacket — a drawing of flowers that Edward recognised as Emma's style. "The guard let me keep this. Emma drew it the day before... before everything changed. She had such a gift for capturing the beauty in simple things."

"And Henry," Thomas' voice softened with pride. "He could never sit still during lessons, but give him a piece of wood and a knife, and he'd work for hours. Made the most intricate little toys."

Edward noted how Thomas straightened his shoulders, as if

the memories themselves lent him strength. The transformation was remarkable — the mere thought of his children bringing colour to his hollow cheeks, life back to his tired eyes.

"They were my light in the darkness," Thomas said. "The thought of holding them again, of making up for these lost years — it kept me going when hope seemed lost."

"And my Mary..." Thomas smiled. "She is such a beauty."

Edward's heart sank. The joy in Thomas' eyes, the way he spoke of Mary as if she still lived — it pierced through him like a knife. He placed a steady hand on Thomas' shoulder.

"Mr Fairchild, there's something you need to know." Edward's voice caught in his throat. "Your wife... she fell ill. She passed away several years ago."

Thomas' legs gave way. He crumpled to the ground, his thin frame shaking with silent sobs. The drawing fluttered from his grasp, and Edward caught it before the wind could take it.

"Your daughter, Mabel — she's remarkable." Edward knelt beside Thomas, pressing the drawing back into his trembling hands. "When Mary fell ill, Mabel took charge. She learned her mother's lace patterns, walked five miles to London each day to sell her work. Even when circumstances forced her to place Emma and Henry in the orphanage, she never stopped fighting to reunite the family."

Thomas' fingers traced the flower pattern on the paper, tears falling onto the faded ink.

Edward gripped Thomas' shoulder tighter. "I give you my word, Mr Fairchild — you will see them again."

SEARCHING

*T*he late afternoon sun cast long shadows across the coaching inn's courtyard as Edward helped Thomas into the carriage bound for Derbyshire. Thomas' gaunt frame and weathered hands betrayed the toll of his imprisonment, yet his eyes held a fierce determination that reminded Edward of Mabel.

"The countryside has changed." Thomas pressed his palm against the window, taking in the newly laid railway tracks cutting through the rolling hills. "Or perhaps I'm the one who's different now."

Edward adjusted the woollen blanket across Thomas' lap. "Time leaves its mark on all things, sir. But what matters most endures."

Thomas sighed. "Six years... My little ones aren't little anymore."

"They've grown into people you'll be proud to know, I am sure." Edward's voice carried warmth and certainty. "Mabel especially. She never lost faith, never stopped fighting for them."

"Like her mother." Thomas traced the faded flowers on the

drawing. "Mary always said Mabel had steel in her spine, wrapped in silk and grace."

The carriage jolted over a rough patch, and Edward steadied Thomas with a gentle hand. "I've seen that strength firsthand."

"But where are they now? What if we can't—" He stopped, shoulders tense with unspoken grief.

Edward leaned forward, meeting Thomas' gaze. "We will find them. I promise."

Thomas nodded slowly. His eyes held both shadow and light — the darkness of years lost, but also the growing spark of hope for reunion.

EDWARD WALKED through Derby's narrow streets, his mind preoccupied with Thomas' hopeful reunion with the children. The late afternoon sun began to set as shop owners began lighting their evening lamps.

Thomas walked behind him. It was clear he was still readjusting to being a free man. His eyes darted around quickly, before quickly dropping to the ground, and his strides were shorter, echoing the times he must have had to shuffle with chains clamped around his ankles.

A glint of white caught Edward's eye. He paused mid-stride, drawn to a shop window where delicate lace pieces hung like frozen snowflakes. The craftsmanship pulled him closer — each thread woven with purpose, each pattern telling its own story. He beckoned Thomas over, and the two men stepped inside the shop.

Thomas raised an eyebrow in questioning, but Edward simply shrugged, and motioned towards the lace pieces.

These weren't the stiff, mechanical designs churned out by London's fashionable establishments. No, these held something more — a grace, a subtle poetry that spoke of careful hands and patient hearts.

"May I help you, sirs?" A shopkeeper stepped forward, his round spectacles catching the lamplight.

Edward barely heard him. His attention fixed on a collar displayed in the centre. The pattern featured winter roses intertwined with forget-me-nots, the same combination he'd seen Mabel sketch during quiet moments at the orphanage. But it was more than the flowers –- it was the way the threads danced together, creating shadows and light that seemed to breathe with life.

His heart quickened as his eyes found the small card beneath: "M. Hampstead Lace."

The memory of Mabel's hands moving over fabric in the dim light of Finch's basement flooded back. The way she'd transformed a wine stain into art at the garden party. Her quiet determination as she worked through nights at the estate, sending money to Emma and Henry.

"This piece..." Edward's voice caught. He cleared his throat. "The artist — M. Hampstead..."

The shopkeeper's eyes lit up. "Ah, you've noticed our finest work. M. Hampstead has transformed this humble shop into quite the destination." He gestured to the other displays. "Started with just a few pieces, but now ladies come from as far as Manchester seeking these designs."

Edward's pulse quickened as the gentleman continued. "She's got six women training under her now. Each brings their own touch to the traditional patterns." The shopkeeper adjusted his spectacles, pride evident in his voice. "Just yesterday, young Nancy mastered the Brussels rose — took to it like she was born with needle in hand. And Eleanor, she's supporting her son's apprenticeship with what she earns."

Thomas gripped the windowsill, his weathered fingers trembling. "My Mabel..." The words came out as a whisper. "She always had her mother's gift."

"Your Mabel?" The shopkeeper's eyebrows shot up.

"Thomas Fairchild, sir. I've..." Thomas' voice cracked. "I've been away."

The man's expression softened with understanding. "She's done you proud, Mr Fairchild. Works through the night sometimes, teaching these women who'd otherwise be headed for the workhouse. Created her own patterns too — see that winter rose there? That's all her design."

Thomas pressed closer to the glass, drinking in every detail of his daughter's work. Joy and anguish battled across his features as he traced the intricate patterns with his gaze. His shoulders shook slightly, and Edward noticed him blinking rapidly.

"She did all this..." Thomas' voice wavered. "While I was..." He couldn't finish the sentence, his hand covering his mouth as tears threatened to spill.

UNITED AGAIN

*T*he door creaked open at Mabel's touch. Her heart stopped. There, on her modest threshold, stood Edward — and beside him, a figure she'd seen only in her dreams these past six years. Her father's weathered face broke into a trembling smile.

"Papa?" The word escaped her lips as a whisper, then transformed into a cry. "Papa!"

She flung herself forward, her arms encircling both men. The rough wool of her father's coat pressed against her cheek, his familiar scent mingling with the sharp winter air. Edward's steady presence anchored them as Thomas' thin frame shook with sobs.

"My girl, my precious girl." Thomas' voice cracked. His hands, once strong from writing on chalkboards, now bore the marks of prison labour as they stroked her hair.

Emma appeared in the doorway, her eyes widening at the sight. She rushed forward, nearly knocking them all off balance. Henry followed, his wooden tools clattering to the floor as he joined the embrace.

Their collective joy filled the small attic room. Henry

pressed his face into Thomas' chest while Emma wrapped her arms around her father's waist. Tears flowed freely as Thomas kissed each of their foreheads, his gaze drinking in their faces.

"You've grown so tall," Thomas marvelled, touching Henry's shoulder. His fingers traced the air near Emma's ear, understanding dawning in his eyes as she watched his lips move.

"We learned to be strong, like you taught us," Mabel said, her voice thick with emotion. She squeezed Edward's hand, drawing him closer into their family circle.

Thomas touched the lace hanging by the window, recognition flickering across his face. "Your mother's patterns... but with your own hand. She would be so proud."

Emma tugged at Thomas' sleeve, showing him the sign language Henry had crafted. Their father's eyes brimmed with fresh tears as his children demonstrated how they'd adapted, survived, and grown together despite their separation.

Laughter bubbled up through their tears as they shared fragments of stories — Henry's clever tools, Emma's detailed drawings, Mabel's growing business. For this precious moment, the pain of their years apart dissolved in the warmth of their reunion.

The joy of reunion settled into a quieter warmth as they gathered around the small table. Emma poured tea while Henry arranged chairs, the familiar domestic rhythm soothing their overwhelmed hearts. But Mabel noticed the shadow crossing Edward's face, the way his shoulders tensed as he glanced between her and her father.

"Mabel... And Mr Fairchild." Edward's voice carried a weight that made Mabel's chest tighten. "There's more you need to know about your imprisonment."

Mabel laid her hand on Edward's arm, feeling the tremor beneath his sleeve. The gesture steadied him, though his eyes held a pain that made her breath catch.

"Your arrest wasn't merely about missing school funds."

Edward's fingers curled around his teacup. "Lady Rowena and Mr Ardon orchestrated your conviction to gain control of your inherited land in Derbyshire. The coal deposits beneath it..." He paused, swallowing hard. "My father's lawyer helped secure the conviction based on evidence Ardon manipulated."

The truth landed like stones in Mabel's stomach. Her fingers dug into Edward's sleeve as the pieces clicked into place. Anger flared hot in her chest, warring with the ache of understanding how deeply the deception had run.

"My family's involvement, though unwitting, contributed to your suffering." Edward's voice cracked. "I discovered the evidence in hospital records — letters between Gerald Houghton and Ardon, payment trails, forged documents. The scheme stretched back years before your arrest."

Mabel's mind reeled. The tablecloth accusation, her dismissal from the estate — it all stemmed from Lady Rowena's desperate attempt to protect her secret. Even her growing feelings for Edward had threatened to unravel the carefully woven web of lies.

Mabel watched her father's weathered hands tighten around his teacup. The revelation of Lady Rowena's scheme had carved new lines into his face, yet his eyes held no bitterness.

"Edward." Thomas' voice carried the same gentle authority she remembered from his teaching days. "You mustn't carry guilt for others' actions. Your kindness to my children, to Mabel especially..." He reached across the table, clasping Edward's shoulder. "That speaks more of your character than any family connection to this betrayal."

The tension in Edward's frame eased slightly under Thomas' touch. Mabel's heart swelled at the quiet understanding passing between the two men.

"We need to expose Lady Rowena's scheme," Edward said, pulling documents from his coat. "These letters, the payment records — they tell the whole story. But my father..." He spread the papers across the table, his fingers tracing the damning signatures. "I want to believe he'll stand for justice once he knows the truth. Yet his pride, his position in society..."

"Your father values honour," Mabel said softly, laying her hand over his. "I saw it during my time at the estate. Even when he took a percentage of my earnings, he did it openly, with clear terms." She met Edward's troubled gaze. "Have faith in that part of him."

Thomas nodded, studying the evidence before them. "Sometimes a man's principles only truly reveal themselves when tested. Lord Montague may surprise us all."

LORD MONTAGUE'S CHOICE

*M*abel's heart thundered against her ribs as they climbed the steps of the Montague estate. The familiar grey stone felt different now — less imposing, more like a fortress built on shifting sand. Edward's hand brushed her elbow, steadying her as Thomas straightened his borrowed coat.

The great oak door swung open, and James' eyes widened at their unexpected arrival. "Master Edward! Miss... Mabel?"

"We need to see my father." Edward's said purposefully. "It's urgent."

Lord Montague sat behind his mahogany desk, his quill paused mid-stroke as they entered his study. Mabel caught the brief flash of displeasure in his eyes at their intrusion.

"Edward. You should have returned a month ago. Your studies finished—"

"Father." Edward spread the documents across the polished wood. "These letters prove Gerald Houghton conspired with Mr Ardon to frame Thomas Fairchild. Our family lawyer helped orchestrate an innocent man's imprisonment."

Lord Montague's face drained of colour as his eyes moved across the damning evidence. His fingers trembled as he lifted a letter bearing Houghton's signature, then another showing payment records to Ardon.

"The coal deposits under the Fairchild property..." Edward's words fell like stones in the silence. "Houghton manipulated evidence, twisted testimony. He used our family's reputation to give weight to false accusations."

Mabel watched Lord Montague's shoulders sag as the truth settled over him. His hand covered his mouth, and for the first time, she saw not the stern lord of the manor, but a man whose foundations had crumbled beneath him.

"My... Our name... our reputation... used to destroy an innocent family." His eyes met Thomas', then dropped to the documents again. Red crept up his neck, and his fingers curled into fists on the desk.

Mabel watched Lord Montague rise from his chair, his face a storm of emotions. He crossed to a cabinet near the window and pulled out a familiar bundle wrapped in brown paper.

"This belongs to your family." He placed Mary's wedding tablecloth in Mabel's hands. The familiar weight of it, the subtle texture of her mother's stitches beneath the paper wrapping, brought tears to her eyes. "I can see now that any claim Lady Rowena makes, cannot be trusted."

Lord Montague turned to Thomas, his proud bearing diminished by the revelation. "Mr Fairchild, no apology can restore the years taken from you. My family's resources were used to destroy yours. I..." His voice caught. "I will ensure every person involved faces justice for their actions."

Thomas' weathered hands trembled as he accepted Lord Montague's outstretched palm. "My lord, I—"

"No." Lord Montague shook his head. "Not 'my lord.' Not after what our reputation cost you." He gripped Thomas' hand firmly. "I will make this right. Lady Rowena, Ardon — they will answer for their crimes. You have my word as a Montague, though I understand if that means little to you now."

Mabel clutched the tablecloth to her chest, feeling the familiar patterns press against her heart. The last piece of her mother, returned at last. She glanced at Edward, who watched his father with quiet pride.

"The truth will be known," Lord Montague continued. "Your name will be cleared publicly, Mr Fairchild. I swear that to you."

THE NET TIGHTENS

*M*abel's fingers traced the familiar patterns of her mother's tablecloth as she arranged displays in the larger front window of their new home on Market Street. The morning light caught the delicate stitches, casting shadows across the wooden floor of what would become their new shop space. Behind her, Henry hammered the last shelf into place while Emma arranged pressed flowers in frames along the walls.

Thomas sat in the corner armchair, his weathered hands holding one of their new account books. His presence still felt like a miracle — watching him trace the numbers, seeing him smile at Emma's drawings, hearing his quiet conversations with Henry about wood types for the display cases.

The knock at the door made her heart leap. Edward stood there, his medical bag in hand, though she knew he hadn't come about patients.

"Father's found more." Edward settled into the chair across from Thomas. "The records keeper at the courthouse remembered Ardon visiting multiple times before your arrest. He saw him meeting with Houghton in private."

Mabel's hands stilled on the lace she'd been arranging. Every piece of news Edward brought felt like another stitch pulling tight, weaving together the truth of what had happened to their family.

"Lord Montague has gathered three magistrates who'll review the evidence." Edward leaned forward, his voice low but steady. "He's traced payments from Houghton to Ardon through a series of bank drafts. Each one dated just before key moments in the trial."

Thomas nodded slowly, his fingers gripping the account book tighter. "And Lady Rowena?"

"Father's advisors are piecing together her involvement. They've found letters between her late husband and Ardon discussing the coal deposits." Edward glanced at Mabel. "The investigation is thorough. Father won't let any detail escape scrutiny."

Mabel returned to her lace arrangement, trying to focus on the delicate patterns rather than the knot of tension in her chest. Each day brought new revelations, new understanding of how carefully their family's destruction had been orchestrated. She caught Emma watching her with concern and managed a small smile, signing that everything was fine.

JUSTICE

*M*abel sat in the crowded courtroom, her heart pounding as she watched Lady Rowena and Mr Ardon stand before the magistrates. The gallery buzzed with whispers — lords and ladies, merchants and maids, all craning their necks to witness the scandal unfold.

Lady Rowena's burgundy silk rustled as she gripped the railing, her composed facade cracking when Edward stepped forward to present the evidence. Her eyes darted between Lord Montague and her former allies, finding no sympathy in their faces.

Mr Ardon's pinched expression had grown even sharper, his shoulders hunched as Edward laid out the documented trail of their deception. Each piece of evidence landed like a physical blow — the bank drafts, the letters, the witness testimonies of their secret meetings.

When Edward spoke, his voice carried through the hushed chamber with unwavering conviction. "My father taught me that a gentleman's duty is to protect those who cannot protect themselves. Yet here we see how position and wealth were utilised to destroy an innocent family."

Mabel watched as Edward gestured to where she sat with Thomas, Emma, and Henry. "Thomas Fairchild served his community as a teacher, shaping young minds with wisdom and care. His daughter Mabel kept her family alive through years of hardship with nothing but her mother's lace patterns and her own determination."

Edward turned to face the magistrates directly. "We cannot allow money and social standing to become shields behind which the powerful can disregard law and human dignity. Every person in this room, regardless of their circumstances, deserves justice. The Fairchilds' suffering proves what happens when we forget this truth."

The gallery erupted in murmurs of agreement. Lady Rowena's face had gone pale, while Mr Ardon seemed to shrink further into himself. Mabel felt Emma's hand slip into hers, squeezing tight as they watched Edward champion their cause before all of London society.

EDWARD STOOD at the window of his father's study, watching raindrops trace paths down the glass. Behind him, Lord Montague's chair creaked as he shuffled through the morning papers.

"The Times has quite the opinion on our family's involvement." Lord Montague's voice carried an edge sharper than usual. He slapped the paper down. "Three columns dedicated to the scandal."

Edward's jaw tightened. "Let them write what they will."

"You realise what this means for the Montague name? For William's political aspirations?"

"I realise what it means for an innocent man who spent six years in prison." Edward turned to face his father. "What would you have had me do? Ignore the evidence? Allow the schemes to continue?"

The words hung between them. Lord Montague paced to the fireplace, gripping the mantle. His shoulders tensed, then slowly dropped.

Edward watched his father's back, the proud shoulders that had always seemed immovable now trembling slightly. The morning light cast long shadows across the study floor between them.

Lord Montague turned. His face, usually a mask of stern authority, cracked with emotion. He crossed the space in three quick strides and pulled Edward into a fierce embrace.

"My son." His father's voice broke. "I am proud — so proud to have raised a man who stands for what's right." His arms tightened around Edward. "Your mother... she would have been proud too. The way you fought for justice, defended those who couldn't defend themselves."

Edward's throat tightened. The mention of his mother, gone these many years, broke something loose inside him. Tears spilled down his cheeks as he gripped his father's coat. Together they wept — for justice served, for bonds renewed, for the spirit of a woman who had taught them both about compassion.

THE AFTERMATH

*L*ady Rowena stared through the rain-streaked window of her sister's northern estate, her reflection a ghostly outline against the gray Yorkshire moors. The familiar weight of her silk dress felt foreign now, like borrowed finery that no longer belonged on her shoulders. Letters from London lay scattered across her writing desk, each one a fresh reminder of her fall from grace.

Her fingers traced the edge of an embossed invitation — one of many that had been rescinded since the trial. The paper crumpled in her grip as she recalled the whispers that had followed her from the courtroom, the turned backs of former friends, the pitying glances from servants who once trembled at her approach.

In the garden below, her sister's children played, their laughter carrying through the glass. She grimaced at how muddy the rain would make them, but that was her sister's problem. One of them made a huge splash as they stomped their way through the puddles that had started to form. They reminded her of Cecilia, who had fled to Bath rather than face the scandal of her mother's disgrace. The distance between them stretched wider than mere miles.

The tea beside her had grown cold, untouched like the stack of visiting cards that no longer arrived. Her sister's household staff moved around her with careful distance, as if her shame might somehow stain their own reputations.

She picked up a small mirror, studying the lines that seemed to have appeared overnight around her eyes. The face that gazed back was still beautiful, still proud, but the calculating gleam that once sparked behind her eyes had dimmed to dull resignation.

A coal fire burned in the grate — coal that might have come from the very deposits she had schemed to possess. The irony of it tasted bitter on her tongue. Her fingers clutched the windowsill as she watched a carriage roll past the gates without turning in, another reminder of her new isolation.

MABEL'S HANDS trembled as she read the notice from the magistrate's office. Edward had brought it over as soon as he had received it.

Mr Ardon would serve his sentence at Maidstone Prison — the same cold walls that had held her father for all those long years. The paper crinkled in her grip as she passed it to her father.

Thomas' weathered fingers brushed against the official seal. "Maidstone," he whispered, his voice thick with memory. The dim light from the shop window cast shadows across his face, highlighting the grey that prison had transformed his dark hair to.

Emma touched her father's arm, her eyes questioning. Henry quickly signed the news to her — their former schoolmaster would face justice in the very place that had stolen their father's freedom. Emma's face lit with understanding, and she wrapped her arms around Thomas' waist.

"It feels strange," Mabel said, watching her father embrace Emma. "To know he'll walk the same corridors, see the same stone walls."

Edward stood by the workbench, his medical bag forgotten at his feet. "The evidence was irrefutable. Every document, every testimony pointed to his deliberate deception." His jaw tightened. "He'll have plenty of time to contemplate the suffering he caused."

"Justice comes in its own time," Thomas said, his voice steady despite the emotion in his eyes. "Though I never expected to see it served in quite this way."

Henry picked up the wooden box containing their mother's wedding tablecloth, running his fingers over the familiar patterns. The lace inside held memories of Mary's hands, her patience, her love — all the things Mr Ardon's cruelty had tried to destroy.

"The truth couldn't stay buried forever," Edward said, moving to stand beside Mabel. "Not with so many lives at stake." His presence steadied her, as it had since those first days at Finch's shop.

Through the window, Mabel watched customers examining the display of "M. Hampstead Lace." Each piece told a story of survival, of beauty created despite darkness. Now those stories held something new — the knowledge that even the deepest wounds could heal when truth finally came to light.

FAIRCHILD LACE

*M*abel looked over the crisp paper of the bank draft. The compensation amount seemed almost surreal – more money than she had ever seen in her life.

Sunlight streamed through the shop window, catching the delicate threads of lace displays. The familiar scent of lavender and beeswax polish filled the air as Mabel sank into her chair, letting the moment settle over her.

Her heart thundered. This sum meant Emma could continue her studies without worry. Henry could pursue his apprenticeship with proper tools and materials. The thought of their futures, once so precarious, now felt solid and real.

The shop bell chimed as Thomas entered from the back room. He carried a stack of ledgers — habit from his teaching days. His eyes met Mabel's, and she saw in them the same mix of disbelief and relief that churned in her own chest.

"I keep expecting to wake up," she admitted, smoothing her apron. The fabric was new, bought just last week — a small luxury she'd finally allowed herself.

"It's real enough." Thomas set the ledgers down, his hands

steady despite the emotion in his voice. "Every penny represents truth finally coming to light."

Mabel nodded, unable to speak past the tightness in her throat. The compensation wasn't just money — it was validation of their years of struggle, of nights spent working by candlelight, of Emma's silent tears and Henry's brave smiles. It acknowledged every sacrifice her mother had made, every moment of faith they'd clung to when hope seemed foolish.

She stood and walked to the window, watching the bustling Derby street outside. Their shop sign caught the morning light — "Fairchild Lace" written in gold leaf. No more hiding, no more shame. The Fairchild name could stand proud again.

CONTENT

*M*abel watched her father's fingers dance across the ledger pages, his handwriting as precise as she remembered from his teaching days. The morning light caught the silver in his hair as he bent over the accounts, but his eyes sparkled with renewed purpose. Each notation was made with the same care he once gave to grading essays.

At the workbench near the window, Emma sat surrounded by scraps of paper covered in intricate drawings. Her latest design incorporated climbing roses with delicate leaves — a pattern that would challenge even Mabel's skilled hands. Emma's fingers moved swiftly as she sketched, pausing occasionally to study the light falling through the lace samples hung nearby.

"Look," Emma signed, holding up her newest creation. The pattern flowed with a natural grace that made Mabel's heart swell. She crossed the room and squeezed Emma's shoulder, nodding in approval at the innovative way Emma had woven traditional elements into something fresh and bold.

The shop door opened, bringing in the scent of sawdust along with Henry. His apprentice apron was covered in wood shavings, and he carried his latest creation wrapped carefully in cloth. Unwrapping it revealed an oval frame of polished oak, its edges carved with delicate ferns that seemed to grow from the wood itself.

"For the winter rose pattern," Henry explained through his signs, positioning the frame against the wall. The craftsmanship showed hours of careful work, each detail considered to complement rather than overshadow the lace it would showcase.

Mabel touched the smooth wood, remembering the little boy who once played with wooden bowls at their breakfast table. Now his strong hands created beauty of their own, his skill growing with each piece he crafted at Master Jenkins' workshop.

The frame would hold Emma's design perfectly, Mabel realised. Their separate arts had found a way to intertwine, creating something greater than any could achieve alone.

Thomas set down his pen and stretched, his shoulders cracking from hours bent over the ledgers. "The accounts are flourishing, Mabel. Your mother would have been proud of what you've built here."

Mabel's throat tightened at the mention of her mother. The shop had become everything she'd dreamed during those dark days at Finch's — filled with light, warmth, and the quiet contentment of women working at their craft. Through the doorway, she glimpsed Nancy showing a new apprentice the basics of Brussels ground stitch, their heads bent together over the pattern.

The late afternoon sun caught the winter rose lace displayed in Henry's frame, casting delicate shadows across the wall. Emma had captured the essence of their mother's technique while adding her own artistic vision. The result drew admirers daily, with orders increasing as word spread through Derby's finest homes.

"We should close early today," Mabel signed to Emma, who nodded and began gathering her sketches. Henry carefully wrapped his tools in leather, each movement precise and practiced.

The familiar routine of closing shop washed over Mabel — checking the day's earnings, securing the valuable lace pieces, and ensuring the workroom was ready for tomorrow's lessons. Her fingers traced the edge of her mother's restored tablecloth, now draped proudly across the display table where all could admire its artistry.

As Thomas helped Emma extinguish the lamps, Mabel caught sight of their reflection in the shop window — father and daughter working in comfortable silence, their movements mirroring each other despite the years apart. The sight filled her chest with warmth.

They stepped out into the cooling evening air, Henry locking the door behind them. The shop sign swayed gently in the breeze.

EDWARD'S HOSPITAL

*M*abel stood in the empty ward of Edward's new hospital, sunlight streaming through tall windows. The space held such possibility — like a blank canvas waiting for purpose. Edward had chosen the old merchant's house well, its broad rooms and high ceilings perfect for transforming into places of healing.

"What do you think?" Edward's voice carried across the wooden floors. He gestured to the rows of iron bed frames they'd arranged that morning. "The light is good, but something's missing."

Mabel ran her hand along a bedpost, remembering the dim corners of Finch's workroom and the workhouse infirmary. "The beds need curtains — not heavy ones that block light, but something to give privacy when needed. And the walls..." She touched the stark plaster. "They're too institutional."

Edward pulled out his notebook, jotting down her observations. "Go on."

"We could hang tapestries between the windows, something soothing to look at during long recoveries. And plants – living things make a space feel less like a sickroom."

He nodded, sketching rough layouts. "The women who come here have seen enough darkness. I want them to feel safe, and cared for."

Mabel moved to the window, studying the courtyard below where workers were clearing overgrown beds. "The garden could provide herbs for medicine, and give patients somewhere peaceful to sit as they recover."

Edward joined her, their shoulders nearly touching. "You understand exactly what I'm trying to create here. Not just a hospital, but a sanctuary." His gray eyes met hers, filled with the same passion she'd seen when he'd broken down Finch's door to save the sick workers.

"I could design some simple lace panels for the windows," Mabel offered. "Something that filters the light without darkening the room. Perhaps a pattern of healing herbs — lavender, chamomile..."

"That would be perfect." Edward's smile warmed her. "Will you help me with the other rooms too? There's still the surgery to arrange, and the recovery spaces..."

Mabel traced her fingers along the windowsill, sketching invisible patterns in her mind. The hospital ward's emptiness held such promise — like her first glimpse of the attic workspace above Mr Bennett's shop. Her heart lifted as she watched Edward measure the distance between beds, his medical precision matching her own attention to detail.

"The light here reminds me of my mother's workroom," she said. "She always said proper light made the difference between good work and great work."

Edward paused his measurements, turning to her with interest. "Tell me more about her methods."

"She arranged her table so the morning light fell just so across her patterns." Mabel demonstrated with her hands. "It revealed every detail, every flaw to be corrected. But it also showed the beauty of what she had and was creating."

"Like diagnosis," Edward said. "The right light helps me see what others might miss." He joined her at the window, their shared understanding filling the space between them.

Mabel pulled out her notebook, adding quick sketches of the ward layout. "Here – if we angle the beds this way, each patient will have both privacy and a view of the garden."

Edward leaned closer, his shoulder brushing hers as he studied her drawings. "You see spaces the way I see patients — as whole beings needing care, not just problems to solve."

His words warmed her. This was different from their cautious interactions at the Montague estate or their desperate collaboration during the orphanage crisis. Here, they worked as equals, each bringing their own expertise to create something meaningful.

"These women deserve dignity in their healing," Mabel said. "Many will come from workrooms like Finch's, or worse." She added details to her sketch — simple screens, small tables for personal items, spaces for flowers.

Edward nodded, making notes in his own journal. "Your experience makes you understand their needs in ways I never could. Together, we can make this place truly serve them."

LORD MONTAGUE'S COMMISSION

*T*he bell above the shop door chimed, and Mabel looked up from her work to find Lord Montague standing in the entrance. His imposing figure cast a long shadow across the wooden floor, but his expression held none of the stern judgment she remembered from their earlier encounters.

"Miss Fairchild." He removed his hat, revealing graying temples. "Your reputation in the village continues to grow."

Mabel set aside her work and stood, smoothing her apron. "My lord, this is unexpected."

"I've watched how your craft brings joy to our community." His eyes swept over the displays of delicate lace. "The church altar needs new cloths for the coming season. I would like to commission you for this work."

Heat rose to Mabel's cheeks. This wasn't just any commission — altar cloths were sacred pieces, meant to honour both God and congregation. "I would be honoured, my lord."

"When it's finished, I want you to deliver it to the church yourself." His voice softened. "It seems fitting."

Mabel's fingers trembled as she reached for her pattern

book. The magnitude of this gesture — Lord Montague choosing her work to grace the church altar — spoke of healing deeper than words could express.

At her workbench that evening, Mabel traced the first patterns onto paper. Her mother had taught her that altar cloths required special attention — each stitch a prayer, each pattern flowing from heart to hands. She incorporated the wild roses that grew in the churchyard, the same ones her mother had pressed between Bible pages.

The lace grew beneath her fingers, delicate as morning frost. She wove in the forget-me-nots that Emma loved to draw, added subtle patterns that spoke of renewal and hope. Every thread carried memories: her mother's patient teachings, prayers whispered over childhood fevers, the quiet strength that had carried them through dark times.

Mabel held the emerging cloth to the light. More than thread and pattern, it would represent their family's journey — from loss to restoration, from shadows to light.

A FUTURE TOGETHER

*M*abel's footsteps carried her and the wrapped altar cloth toward the village church. Her heart quickened with each step, memories flooding back of Sunday mornings when Mama guided her small hand to make the sign of the cross. The spire rose against the morning sky, sunlight catching the weathered stone just as it had in her childhood.

The heavy wooden door creaked open beneath her touch. Inside, dust motes danced in shafts of coloured light that poured through the stained glass windows. The scent of beeswax and incense wrapped around her, unchanged since the days she'd knelt beside her mother in the third pew, learning to fold her hands in prayer.

The altar cloth felt warm against her chest as she walked down the centre aisle. Movement caught her eye — a figure stood near the front, tall and familiar. Edward. He turned toward her, and in his hands lay something delicate and white. A pattern, she realised, watching lace cascade over his arm in graceful folds. Even from this distance, she recognised Emma's distinctive touch in the design — the way the flowers seemed to dance across the fabric, alive with possibility.

Their gazes met across the sacred space. In that moment, every step of their journey seemed present: the basement of Finch's shop, the orphanage, the fever ward, the fight for justice. Understanding passed between them, deep and wordless as prayer itself.

Edward held up the intricate lace pattern as he took a step towards Mabel. Her heart skipped at the sight of Emma's distinctive flower motifs woven throughout — the same wild roses that had decorated her childhood sketchbooks.

"Mabel, I've designed this with Emma's help," Edward's voice carried through the empty church, thick with emotion. "And I want to ask if you will join me on this journey, building a life together."

The sunlight streaming through the stained glass caught the glint of metal as Edward lowered himself to one knee. From beneath the lace, he revealed a ring that sparkled with quiet dignity. "Miss Fairchild. Will you marry me?"

Mabel's breath caught in her throat. The weight of their different worlds pressed against her chest — his life of privilege and her years of struggle, the society balls and the workhouse floor. Yet as she met Edward's gaze, she saw only the man who had broken down Finch's door to save the sick, who had raced through winter storms to help her siblings, who had fought to free her father despite his own family's involvement.

The love radiating from his eyes spoke of something deeper than social station or family name. It whispered of shared dreams — of healing and teaching, of creating beauty from pain, of building bridges between the worlds they'd both inhabited.

"Edward, before I answer, there's something you must understand." She squared her shoulders, drawing strength from the memory of her mother's final words. "My family — Emma, Henry, and Father — their needs must always remain a priority. I cannot abandon them, not after everything we've endured."

The morning light caught Edward's face as his expression

shifted from anxious anticipation to pure joy. His eyes crinkled at the corners, and his smile spread wide across his features.

"My dearest Mabel, your devotion to family is one of the countless reasons I love you." He reached for her hand, his touch warm and sure. "Their well-being will be our shared purpose. Together, we can create a life that honours both love and duty."

Relief flooded through Mabel's chest, releasing a tension she hadn't realised she carried. Her heart swelled with certainty as she met his gaze.

"Yes, Edward. Yes, I will marry you."

The words hung in the air between them, simple and profound. Sunlight streamed through the stained glass, casting patterns of blue and gold across the stone floor where they stood. In this sacred space that held so many memories of her childhood prayers, Mabel felt the rightness of their connection — forged through trials, strengthened by shared purpose.

The lace in Edward's hands caught the light, each carefully crafted stitch representing hours of work and love. Emma's wild roses danced alongside traditional patterns, just as their two worlds had merged. Mabel's heart filled with warmth at the thought of their partnership, knowing that together they could build something greater than themselves.

Mabel lifted the altar cloth with reverent hands, its weight familiar yet different in this sacred space. The intricate patterns caught the morning light streaming through the windows, casting delicate shadows across the polished wood. As she draped it across the altar, each stitch seemed to whisper stories — of her mother's teachings, Emma's artistic touch, and the countless hours spent perfecting every detail. The cloth represented more than mere decoration; it embodied their shared dreams of healing and unity.

Edward stepped closer, his presence warm beside her. His eyes traced the patterns she'd woven — herbs for healing, roses for love, and forget-me-nots for family bonds. The pride in his gaze matched the gentle way he'd handled her lace designs for the hospital windows. Here, in this quiet sanctuary, her art transformed the space just as their partnership would transform lives.

Their fingers intertwined as they turned from the altar. Mabel's ring caught the light, sending tiny sparkles dancing across the stone floor. Together, they walked down the aisle toward the heavy wooden doors. Outside, sunlight bathed the churchyard in golden warmth, highlighting the wild roses that had inspired so many of her patterns.

Standing on the church steps, the challenges ahead seemed less daunting with Edward's hand in hers. She knew that every decision they made would consider Emma's continued education, Henry's flourishing apprenticeship, and her father's recovery. Their love had grown from this foundation of family devotion, and it would continue to strengthen as they built their future together.

PROMISES

Sunlight poured through the stained glass windows of the village church, casting jewelled patterns across the worn stone floor. The smell of beeswax candles and fresh flowers filled the air as guests settled into the wooden pews. Whispers and rustles echoed through the space.

Thomas stood beside her in the church vestibule, his weathered hands steady as he adjusted her veil. The years of separation melted away in this moment — his presence beside her felt like a miracle born of perseverance and faith. When he offered his arm, Mabel caught a glimpse of the proud teacher he'd once been, standing straighter despite the lingering effects of his imprisonment.

"Ready, my dear?" Thomas' voice carried the warmth of summer afternoons spent reading poetry in their old cottage.

Emma stepped forward, radiant in her maid of honour dress. The lace trim along her sleeves showcased her growing mastery of the craft — each stitch expressing love and dedication. Her smile spoke volumes as she signed her joy, her fingers dancing with the grace that had transformed her silence into its own form of music. The sisters shared a look that contained years of shared struggles and triumphs.

Henry moved to his place among the groomsmen, his new suit fitting perfectly across shoulders that had grown strong from his woodworking apprenticeship. Pride shone in his eyes as he took his position, standing tall as a young man rather than the frightened boy from the orphanage.

The familiar notes of the wedding hymn filled the church. Thomas squeezed Mabel's arm gently as they prepared to walk down the aisle. Through the doorway, she could see Edward waiting, his face bright with love and promise.

Through the church doorway, Mabel caught sight of Lord Montague seated in the front pew. His stern countenance had softened, and he nodded with quiet dignity as their eyes met. Beside him, Clara beamed, her green eyes bright with unshed tears of joy. She'd arranged white roses along the pews herself that morning, insisting on personally overseeing every detail of the decoration.

The transformation in Lord Montague struck Mabel deeply. Gone was the cold dismissal from that terrible day in his study. Instead, his presence carried the weight of reconciliation, of bridges mended through truth and understanding. He'd even insisted on providing the wedding breakfast, though Mabel had initially demurred.

Clara rose slightly from her seat as Mabel passed, reaching out to brush her hand in a gesture of sisterly affection. Their friendship had blossomed in unexpected ways since those first days when Mabel served as her lady's maid. Now Clara managed the household accounts for Mabel's growing lace school, bringing her business acumen to bear in ways that made both families stronger.

The sight of Lord Montague and Clara sitting among her students from the lace school, the women she'd trained who now formed an honour guard along the aisle, filled Mabel's heart. Mr Bennett stood proudly near the back, his shop window having given her work its first real chance. Mrs Winters from the orphanage dabbed at her eyes with a handkerchief edged in Mabel's distinctive winter rose pattern.

These people — from both worlds she'd inhabited — had become more than mere witnesses. They represented the threads of her life, woven together like the intricate patterns she created, each adding strength and beauty to the whole. Their presence transformed what could have been a simple ceremony into a testament to how love could bridge any divide.

The women Mabel had trained lined the aisle, their faces glowing with pride. Nancy Warner stood tall, her once-trembling hands now steady as she held a length of exquisite Brussels lace. Eleanor Cooper's eyes shone with tears, the memory of her first fumbling stitches replaced by the masterful collar she'd created for her son's apprenticeship ceremony.

Each woman carried a piece of lace she'd crafted, holding them high to form an archway of intricate patterns. Mary-Beth's winter roses bloomed alongside Alice's climbing vines, their designs flowing together like a garden caught in thread. The delicate pieces caught the light streaming through the windows, casting lacework shadows across the stone floor.

Mabel's heart swelled as she walked beneath their work. These women had come to her broken by circumstances, much as she had arrived at Finch's shop years ago. Now they stood transformed — not just by the skills they'd learned, but by the community they'd built together. Their weekly gatherings had become more than lessons in technique; they'd become a sanctuary where women lifted each other up, shared in each other's triumphs, supported each other through hardships.

Thomas guided her to the altar where Edward waited. His eyes met hers with the same warmth she'd felt that day in Finch's shop, when he'd helped gather scattered medical journals from the floor. He took her hands in his, steady and sure.

They spoke their vows in clear voices that carried to the rafters. Edward promised to honour her family's needs alongside their own. Mabel pledged her heart while acknowledging the broader family they'd built together — one that included her students, his patients, and all those their united work would touch.

When Edward's lips met hers, sealing their promises, the women raised their lace pieces higher, creating a canopy of beauty above the newly married couple. The intricate patterns danced with light and shadow, a testament to how far they'd all come together.

THE FIRST CHAPTER OF 'THE WORKHOUSE ORPHAN'S REDEMPTION'

*T*he gas lamps flickered to life as dusk settled over London, casting long shadows across the cobblestone streets. Emma Grace Redbrook clutched her father's hand, her wide hazel eyes drinking in the sights and sounds of the bustling city. The clip-clop of horses' hooves mingled with the shouts of street vendors, creating a symphony of urban life that both thrilled and overwhelmed the ten-year-old girl.

"Papa, look!" Emma tugged on John's sleeve, pointing at a

peddler balancing an array of shiny pots and pans on his shoulders. "How does he carry all that?"

John chuckled, his laugh lines deepening. "Years of practice, I'd wager."

Mary placed a gentle hand on Emma's shoulder, steering her away from a passing carriage that splashed muddy water onto the pavement. "Mind where you're walking, love."

Emma nodded, but her attention was already captured by a group of street urchins huddled around a storyteller, their faces alight with wonder. She longed to join them, to lose herself in tales of far-off lands and daring adventures.

As they turned onto Whitechapel High Street, Emma noticed a change in the air. The excitement of moments before gave way to a palpable tension. Hushed whispers passed between shopkeepers as they hurriedly shuttered their windows. A crowd had gathered around a wall where a man was nailing up a notice, his face grim.

"What's happening, Mama?" Emma asked, pressing closer to Mary's side.

Her mother's grip tightened. "Nothing to worry about, my dear. Just some city business."

But Emma couldn't shake the feeling that something was very wrong. She caught snatches of conversation as they passed:

"...another case on Brick Lane..."

"...closing the pump on Broad Street..."

"...cholera's back, God help us all..."

The word 'cholera' sent a shiver down Emma's spine, though she didn't fully understand its meaning. She looked up at her parents, noting the worry lines etched on their faces, so at odds with their reassuring smiles.

Emma's heart raced as her father's cough echoed through the narrow street. She glanced up at him, worry creasing her young brow. John's face had gone pale, his shoulders hunched as he fought to catch his breath. Mary's hand tightened on Emma's shoulder, a silent comfort that did little to ease the knot forming in her stomach.

"Perhaps we should hurry home," Mary said.

As they neared their modest dwelling, Emma's eyes darted to the small bakery on the corner. The warm, yeasty smell of fresh bread wafted through the air, momentarily chasing away her fears.

"Mama," she said, tugging gently on Mary's sleeve. "May I fetch some bread? And... perhaps a bit of honey?"

Mary hesitated, her gaze flicking between John and Emma. After a moment, she nodded, fishing out a few carefully hoarded pennies from the pocket sewn into her apron. "Be quick about it, love."

Emma clutched the coins tightly, their edges biting into her palm as she hurried into the bakery. The shopkeeper's smile didn't quite reach his eyes as he wrapped a small loaf and dolloped honey into a twist of paper. Emma thanked him, cradling her precious cargo as she rushed back to her parents.

The climb up the narrow staircase to their rooms seemed steeper than usual. Emma's breath caught in her throat as she pushed open the door to find her mother helping her father into bed. His cough had worsened, each ragged breath sending a shudder through his frame.

"Papa?" Emma's voice quavered.

Mary turned, forcing a smile. "Your father just needs some rest, dear. Why don't you read to him for a bit? It always soothes him so."

Emma nodded, setting aside the bread and honey. She retrieved her most prized possession – a small, well-worn Bible – from its hiding place beneath a loose floorboard. Settling into the chair beside her father's bed, she opened to the Book of Psalms, his favourite.

"The Lord is my shepherd," Emma began, her young voice steady despite the fear coiling within her. "I shall not want..."

Click here to read the rest of 'The Workhouse Orphan's Redemption'

Faith. Defiance. A Love Forged in Fire.

In the brutal world of Victorian London, Emma Redbrook's life begins in tragedy. Orphaned and trapped in Grimshaw's Workhouse, she endures cruelty that would break most spirits. But Emma's unwavering faith becomes her beacon of hope — and her strength.

When a daring escape leads her into the city's treacherous underworld, Emma must navigate a landscape of danger and survival. Her childhood friend Thomas — once her closest ally — has been transformed by years of hardship into a man she barely recognises.

As London trembles on the brink of industrial revolt, Emma finds herself caught between loyalty and justice. Can she prevent a catastrophe that threatens to consume everything she loves? Will Thomas remember the hope they once shared? And at what cost will she fight for her principles?

From the grim workhouse to the glittering world of the wealthy, Emma's journey will test the limits of faith, love, and human resilience. Can one woman's courage truly change the course of destiny? Will love and hope triumph over despair?

'The Workhouse Orphan's Redemption'

without sex or swearing, but with all of the mystery and romance you expect from a great story.

Be the first to know when we release new books, take part in our fun competitions, and get surprise free books in your inbox by signing up to our free VIP Reader list.

As a thank you you'll receive a copy of 'The Little Orphan Waif's Crusade' straight away, alongside other gifts.

Click here to sign up for our mailing list, and receive your FREE stories.

CornerstoneTales.com/sign-up

LOVE VICTORIAN ROMANCE?

Other Rachel Downing Books

The Workhouse Orphan's Redemption

In the brutal world of Victorian London, Emma Redbrook's life begins in tragedy. Orphaned and trapped in Grimshaw's Workhouse, she endures cruelty that would break most spirits. But Emma's unwavering faith becomes her beacon of hope — and her strength.

Get 'The Workhouse Orphan's Redemption' Here!

The Orphan's Christmas Hymn

Seven-year-old Clara Winters' world shatters when tragedy strikes days before Christmas. Sent to St. Mary's Church Orphanage, she finds her only solace in the hymns that once filled her happy home. When her angelic voice catches the attention of the kind-hearted Reverend Thornton and his musically gifted son Edward, Clara dares to dream of a brighter future.

Get 'The Orphan's Christmas Hymn' Here!

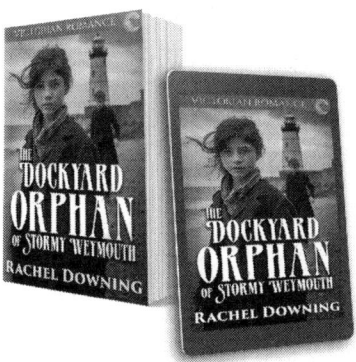

The Dockyard Orphan of Stormy Weymouth

Sarah Campbell's world crumbles when a tragic accident claims her parents' lives. She finds solace in the lighthouse's beam that guides ships to safety. But it's a young fisherman wrestling with his own loss, who truly captures her heart.

Get 'The Dockyard Orphan of Stormy Weymouth' Here!

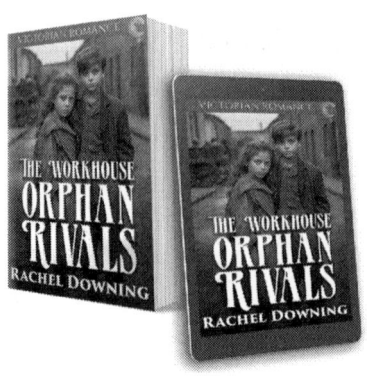

The Workhouse Orphan Rivals

Childhood sweethearts torn apart. A promise broken. A love that refuses to die.

Get 'The Workhouse Orphan Rivals' Here!

The Orphan Prodigy's Stolen Tale

When ten-year-old Isabella Farmerson's world shatters with the tragic loss of her parents, she's thrust into a life of hardship and uncertainty.

Get 'The Orphan Prodigy's Stolen Tale' Here!

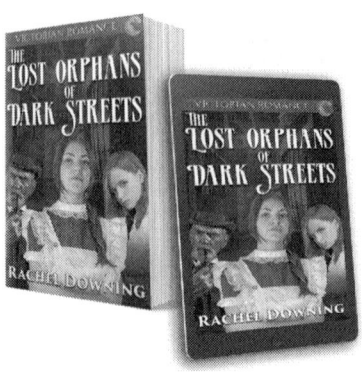

The Lost Orphans of Dark Streets

Follow the stories of Elizabeth and Molly as they negotiate the dangerous slums and find their place in the world.

Get 'The Lost Orphans of Dark Streets' Here!

Two Steadfast Orphan's Dreams

Follow the stories of Isabella and Ada as they overcome all odds and find love.

Get 'Two Steadfast Orphan's Dreams' Here!

And from our other Victorian Romance Author Dorothy Wellings...

The Moral Maid's Unjust Trial

Matilda must fend for herself when her father is wrongfully accused for a crime he didn't commit.

Get 'The Moral Maid's Unjust Trial' Here!

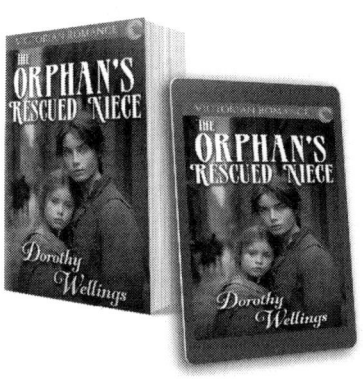

The Orphan's Rescued Niece

As Beatrice grows from a wide-eyed child into a resilient young woman, she finds herself caught between her love for her troubled brother and her desire for a life free from poverty and fear.

Get 'The Orphan's Rescued Niece' Here!

If you enjoyed this story, sign up to our mailing list to be the first to hear about our new releases and any sales and deals we have.

We also want to offer you a Victorian Romance novella - 'The Little Orphan Waif's Crusade' - absolutely free!

Click here to sign up for our mailing list, and receive your FREE stories.

CornerstoneTales.com/sign-up

Printed in Dunstable, United Kingdom